# AUNT ELLIE TURNS SLEUTH

# AUNT ELLIE TURNS SLEUTH

*A Novel*

**Liz Clarke**

iUniverse, Inc.
New York Lincoln Shanghai

**AUNT ELLIE TURNS SLEUTH**



iUniverse books may be ordered through booksellers or by contacting:

iUniverse
2021 Pine Lake Road, Suite 100
Lincoln, NE 68512
www.iuniverse.com
1-800-Authors (1-800-288-4677)



ISBN: 978-0-595-47632-9 (pbk)
ISBN: 978-0-595-91896-6 (ebk)

Printed in the United States of America

## MAJOR CHARACTERS

ON SITE:

Eleanor (Ellie) Lee—Aunt who raised Shell Lee McGivern

Kathryn Banks—Ellie's friend

Christopher (Chris) Marchand—Police Officer

Dr. Richard Banks—Kathryn's brother

Norma Banks—his wife

Deeanna Banks—their daughter.

Judge Anthony Essex—friend

Helen Essex—his wife

Susan Gianelli—whose father was murdered

Eva Gianelli—Susan's step-mother

Lewis Howard—friend and employee of murder victim

And other incidental characters.

ON CALL:

Shell Lee McGivern (now Sheppard)

Patrick Abrams (Shell's private investigator) a/k/a "Abe"

Moira Abrams (retired detective, now working part time for son "Abe")

Mutt was tugging persistently on his leash. He didn't want to go where I wanted to go—but what the heck? We had plenty of time to explore where his nose was leading him, and still wander over to the duck pond later.

This little park had become one of my favorite places since I'd moved to Charlotte to live with Kathryn. We'd purchased a house not far away and Mutt and I came here to walk almost every morning, me with a couple of plastic bags in my pocket. The Park Board discouraged leaving unwanted 'deposits' behind, and besides, it wasn't good manners.

I'd been raised with good manners. Mother would have been appalled at any slip-ups from anybody living under her jurisdiction, and that included Pops. He'd simply raise one eyebrow, then wink at me, when she corrected me or my older sister, Anna, or later, Anna's daughter, Shell. She'd died when Shell was nine years old, so the kid didn't get as much scolding as everyone else. She'd turned out pretty good anyway, if I shouldn't say so myself, since I'd had most of the raising of her.

Thus far this morning both bags were still in my pocket, but if Mutt was just looking for an appropriate dumping ground, one would soon be in use, so I followed him off the path.

That's when our beautiful morning turned disastrous. Mutt had his nose on the body before I could drag him off. Darn dog is almost too strong for me, but he was what I'd wanted. Kathryn wanted to buy me some expensive fancy breed, but I'd seen Mutt in the shelter and we'd fallen in love with each other, so for $50, signing about ten times in my own blood, taking the secret oath, learning the password and secret handshake with a promise he'd get to the Vet within four days and eventually be neutered, he'd come home with me.

He was some kind of Heinz mixed breed and even as a pup we knew he was going to be huge, but he was gorgeous anyway, at least in my eyes.

Now he didn't want to abandon his 'find' and it was difficult to pull him away.

My first thought was "What would Shell do?" Of course the obvious answer was to dial 911. Kathryn had insisted that I always carry my cell phone if I went out alone, so I quickly dug it from my pocket (the one without the plastic baggies) and dialed.

Having given my information and location, and the fact that I was NOT calling from my home number, but on a cell, I sat down on the ground to wait.

Big Mistake! It was still very early in the morning and the grass was extremely damp from excessive dew. I was probably going to end up giving my statement at the Police Station with the seat of my jeans wet. Couldn't be helped. My legs were caving in under me and I knew I couldn't continue to stand there and wait for help to arrive. Better to have wet pants!

Mother, of course, wouldn't have agreed. One's dignity must be maintained at all costs. Pop raised his eyebrow and winked. I know he did. I saw him.

Mutt had finally given up his struggle to return to his discovery, and I pulled him to me, hugged him and buried my face in his soft fuzzy neck. The veterinarian we'd taken him to has ventured a guess that there was "some Springer Spaniel" in him, and possibly some Great Dane which contributed to both his soft curly fur and his size. What else he might be was known to nobody but God. If He knew.

My Aunt Dora, at whose home I'd spent a lot of my childhood, mooching cookies from her never-ending cookie jar, would have said, "For shame, Eleanor, God knows everything." Of course, she knew personally, because she prayed all the time, and somewhere along the line He'd have told her so. And I believed Aunt Dora.

So I know this because she told me so. No matter what subject came up, and she talked almost constantly, it always ended up, "And I prayed about it and the Lord told me … (whatever)".

I've thought about this a lot and finally decided she was right, only my conclusion is that since He gave us the brain to ask questions with, He also gave us the brain to figure out the answer. The only problem is that most of us try to take credit for all our so-called personal decisions, and Aunt Dora didn't.

Now I decided to ask: "Why us, Mutt?" and my answer came back: "Why not us?" I must have said this aloud, because Mutt licked my face, which I guess is his way of consoling me when I'm distressed.

"Thanks, Mutt," I whispered into his silky ear, "Better us than some little child stumbling upon a scene like this. But I do wish somebody would get here soon."

As if in answer to my prayer, sirens could be heard approaching, and soon a voice called out, "Miss Lee, where are you?"

"Just down the path a little more, and off to your right," I called back. I wasn't about to try to get up and locate him. I'd probably fall on my face and totally disgrace myself. "Wuss," I told myself, "You should have more backbone. Shell would have."

But of course, Shell was not only my niece, she's a former policewoman and also had a number of serious problems befall her since she inherited Rayburn Enterprises, including attempts on her life, and a number of murders to solve. I reassured myself that I didn't need her strength and gumption, but the queasy feeling that I was somehow less than courageous just wouldn't abate.

The young man who approached patted Mutt on the head. I had the distinct feeling that he felt like doing the same for me, but protocol and convention prevented it. Too bad, really. I felt like I could use a good friendly pat, anywhere that was appropriate of course.

"You said you found a body?" he asked.

"Yes. Well, not me, exactly. Mutt discovered it. I was just being dragged along."

I pointed in the direction of the body, as he said, "The EMTs are on the way. But It seems what we really need is the Coroner and a Forensics team, right?"

"Probably," I replied "I'm really not very well informed on the subject, in spite of all the CSI and Forensics shows on TV."

"Most people aren't," he reassured me. "That's what the professionals are for. You just sit there while I go check this out."

He disappeared, and more sirens could be heard.

A lot of people arrived, in various types of vehicles, bearing all kinds of 'stuff'—yellow tape, medical bags and life-saving equipment, unneeded of course, and cameras.

Out of sight from the body, I could hear them, and see flashes of light. Totally out of context, all I could think of was "lights, camera, action" as it seemed like something out of a bad movie. One I wouldn't want to go see.

There was a lot of tramping around, but eventually they began, one vehicle at a time, to leave, until finally there was only Mutt, myself, the first young officer who'd arrived, and a lot of yellow tape.

He now reached down to help me up, saying, "Sorry, ma'am but I've been asked to escort you down to Police Headquarters so you can give your statement."

"Okay," I said, "I figured as much. Can you tell me what happened?"

"Stabbed apparently," he said. "Not a nice way to go."

"Weapon?"

"Couldn't find any. Perp apparently either tossed it far away, or took it with him. We searched the perimeter, but will send some people back to re-check the area."

Once on my feet, I found, to my surprise, that I actually could move. Mutt could too. He was, in fact, more than anxious to resume our walk, but of course we couldn't do that.

And YES, my bottom was more than damp. The young man noticed and asked, "Is your car nearby? Do you want to go home and change?"

"We walked, but yes, I'd like to get some dry clothes if that's possible, and toss these in the laundry."

I turned my back to him, pointing to my rear, and he said, "Yep, Grass stains, too. Mom would say you'd better get them soaking as soon as possible. I wouldn't know. Helpless at that kind of thing. Well, at least you dried off some of the dew. Dog's tummy is pretty wet too. I'll just run you home, you can leave him there before we head for the Station."

I said, "We'll get your car seats damp."

"That's okay. There are a couple of blankets in the trunk we can put down. Wanna wash and dry them too?" He laughed, easing the tension.

"Sure. That'll be your reward for being so nice."

We left Mutt in the back yard, which was already fenced in when we bought the place, on account of the pool, while I got more appropriately dressed and put my jeans in the washing machine. I still hadn't become accustomed to the idea that water could be wasted. All those years at home, on a retiree's (Pop's) low budget, we'd wait until we had a full load before turning it on. The same thing applied to the dishwasher (one of our few luxuries). Of course I turned the dial to 'small load' to ease my conscience.

In all the years we'd raised Shell, I didn't realize the entire truth about our so-called budget, or I wouldn't have worried, or skimped quite so much, but I'll tell you about that later.

Now it was time to face the statement I'd have to make to the Police. Actually there wasn't much I could say, since there wasn't much I KNEW!

Upon leaving the Police Station, I found the same young officer, whose name I now knew to be Christopher (just call me Chris) Marchand, waiting at the door with instructions to take me home.

I had other ideas. I had to get to Kathryn and dump my woes on her. I don't recall how many times I've done that, or how many times I've cried on her sympathetic shoulder. I told him where I was going and assured him I had a means of getting home, when I was ready to go. I also made him promise to keep on top of the investigation and keep me informed as to what was happening.

I sailed through Kathryn's office, past desks and office staff without even a glance or 'hi' to any of them. This was unusual, since I'd become friends with most of them since moving to Charlotte.

Kathryn's personal secretary, seated just outside her door, rose to let me in, but I just pushed past her and ran in. She simply backed off and closed the door after me.

I collapsed into a chair, exclaiming, "Oh, KAT!"

Nobody but me gets to call her that, and I don't know why she lets me get away with it. I'd started it years ago, and I knew she'd soon come to recognize it as a term of endearment, but even Heaven couldn't help anybody else who tried it.

Oddly enough, the name fits her, with her sleek dark hair (which would have more than a few white strands in if she'd permit them) and her quick, silent movements. Even her chair didn't dare squeak as she slipped out of it and came around to me, recognizing my distress.

If we'd been at home I knew she'd have put her arms around me, but this was her capital 'O' Office, and would remain relatively formal. No unrecognized visitors or new clients ever got past the vigilante at the reception desk. All the staff came and went wherever and whenever they pleased, and who knew which of them might come wandering in.

Now she just leaned back against the front of her desk and stood there, waiting. Not until I'd blurted out the entire story did she offer the comfort of her shoulder. But not before locking the office door!

All this happened and it wasn't even lunch time. This was JUST TOO MUCH! I didn't want to even think about what the rest of the day might bring.

I said so, and Kat, knowing I couldn't skip a meal (I'm just like my niece, Shell, in that regard—I really can't understand why we both manage to maintain our weight), decided it was time to take me to lunch.

I declined, eyes red from crying, "I'm not very presentable. Let's just go home and I'll fix something. There's left-over ham and potato salad in the refrigerator we need to get rid of. Besides, doing something useful would probably help get me back on track, and I'll stop falling apart on you. Okay?"

"Whatever you want, girl." she said.

We went home.

Mutt was tugging persistently on his leash.

If you think I've either lost my mind, or my computer literacy and accidentally returned to line one, page one, you are only partly right.

Even I realize that returning immediately to the scene of the crime makes me somewhat out of my mind.

I rationalized it by telling myself it was like the old theory of falling off a horse and getting right back on him.

I'd fed myself and Kathryn, and brought Mutt in from the back porch. He didn't have a dog house. We had a large sunporch on the back of the house. One end was my potting table and storage for garden tools, bags of potting soil, extra clay pots, a large old kitchen sink, etc. Between the carpenter and the plumber, I had a great place to work. The other end of the porch had two lounge chairs and a small table, and we'd just added a large doggie door and his bed. Kathryn said he probably had the largest doghouse in the county. When he wanted all the way into the house he just sat there and whined. He'd already learned he was NOT to scratch on the door!

Kat wanted to stay with me, but I insisted she return to work. The everyday chore of fixing lunch had gotten me back to feeling relatively normal, and I didn't want to be pampered.

When she'd gone, I phoned my niece, Shell, re-told my story for the third time and asked her advice.

"*Keep out of it.*" was basically what I'd been told.

"Why?"

"*Because you aren't either emotionally or physically equipped for P.I. work.*"

Now she had me royally miffed! "Is that all?" I asked.

"*No, sweetie,*" she said, *"It's a job for the cops. Let them handle it. You could get yourself hurt, and I'd be really mad at you if you did that."*

"I hear ya." I replied.

Okay, so being miffed took precedence over advice, or common sense, and here we were, Mutt and I, back at the scene of the murder. I refuse to say 'alleged' murder, since Chris had admitted no weapon had been found.

I wasn't even real sure of the cause of death. Chris has said probably a knife. I'd seen a lot of blood, and Mutt had gotten his nose in it. Even in my uninformed mind, all that blood seemed to eliminate either poison, strangulation, or some natural cause such as a heart attack.

The yellow crime scene tape was gone already, so apparently the police had given up, having searched, bagged, photographed, and whatever else they do.

The only evidence that a crime had been committed here was the flattened grass, both from where the body had lain, and from the trampling of numerous feet, plus blood still on the grass.

Mutt had started there, but was pulling me to the south, nose to the ground.

A voice behind me asked, "Miss Lee, what are you doing back here?"

"Snooping, obviously," I said to Chris. "What about yourself?"

"The same. How about him?" pointing to Mutt. "What's his take on this? Is part of the Heinz mix bloodhound? Or does he just think it is?"

"Don't know," I said, "But he seems to want to lure us off this direction."

"Then let's take his word for it and follow along."

"I have every intention of doing just that."

We followed, and he said, "You seem to have recovered."

"Yep," was my answer. "A good cry plus lunch will do that. But it's probably because I'm angry."

"At what? Not at me, I hope."

"Well, first of all, somebody messed with my morning walk. Second, I had a small disagreement with my niece, who ordered me to cease and desist. She doesn't take orders well herself, and I just learned that I don't either. She made me mad, inferring that I was helpless and incapable of.... oh, I don't know what of. Taking care of myself, I guess. I raised her from infancy through college, and now she thinks.... well, I guess I don't really know what she thinks. I just know she would have been back here herself, looking things over, trying to see anything that had been missed.

"So Mutt and I talked it over and decided to come back, me to face my fears, him to finish his walk, do his duty somewhere other than our back yard, and see what else he might discover."

He said, "So you're second guessing us? The Police force, I mean?"

"Uh, huh," I said, "No offense."

"I'm not offended. Beautiful ladies aren't stupid just because they are pretty."

"Flattery will only get you the privilege of picking up after Mutt," I said, handing him one of the little baggies and pointing to a small brown pile where Mutt had stopped briefly during his search.

Chris laughed, did as instructed, tossing the 'evidence' in a nearby trash can, and we continued following the determined pup into some weeds. I was beginning to accumulate some of those little burrs that are so pesky, and knew I was going to be spending time picking them off and grooming Mutt when I got him home.

Just then the dog began scratching in the dirt. Chris quickly grabbed the leash and pulled him back. "Hang onto him, Miss Lee," he said, "If he's found something there than some other dog's buried lunch, I'd better check. It does appear that the ground there has been disturbed a little."

While I restrained my friendly, fuzzy, four-footed friend, Chris brushed away some loose dirt, then said, "Got another of those baggies? I don't seem to have any gloves with me. Stupidly left them in my car."

I handed him another bag and he was soon tugging on something. Holy Dog Treats! It looked like the handle of a knife!

He laid it on the ground and said, "I'd better call this in. You and Mutt may have been right to question our thoroughness. In the meantime, we'd all better get back from here with as few tracks as possible." He literally picked Mutt up, which isn't easy, and we both stepped away.

He phoned it in. I sat down to wait—again—but this time at least the grass was dry.

Chris remained standing, leaning against a nearby tree. "So," he asked, "have you had the dog long?"

"Several months," I replied, "have you had that curly blonde hair and violet eyes very long?"

"Fair question. Almost twenty-nine years. Why? And do I get to ask how long you've had yours?"

"No."

"Okay. Then what do we discuss while we wait for my Super to get here?"

"We discuss your curly blonde hair and violet eyes, I guess," I replied.

"And do I get to ask why?"

"Because you remind me so much of my niece. You look a lot like her, except that there's not one ounce of feminine traits to you. And she's a former policewoman."

"Former?" he asked, "Why did she leave the force?"

"Inherited a ranch in Wyoming and moved. Then her Chief, also now referred to as a 'former' followed her out there, sensing trouble in the e-mails she was sending to a friend, who just happened to be the combined office secretary and dispatcher in the same office."

"Were his instincts correct?"

"Totally. He got there in time to save her from being murdered."

"Wow! That sounds like a story. Then what happened?"

"They got married, live at the ranch, and now have one child."

"Well, Miss, I hope the story ends with 'lived happily ever after.'"

"Should. Provided he doesn't kill himself in that airplane."

He said, "The story gets bigger, I take it?"

"Quite a bit longer at least. Maybe someday if I get to know you better I'll tell it all."

We started hearing the now familiar sirens and two vehicles arrived simultaneously. This time I wasn't required to go to the Police Station, since Chris had been the one who actually dug up the knife.

He explained, "I was just cruising the area, as instructed, to watch for anything suspicious, when Miss Lee and Mutt came walking in again, bold as a pair of pesky mosquitoes. I refuse to apologize for that, Miss Lee, but really you shouldn't have been here."

"But aren't you glad we were?"

"Guilty as charged," he said, "Anyway, I parked and followed them. The dog had his nose to the ground, pretending to be a bloodhound, and he's the one who led us to the knife, which was partially buried. Looked as though it had been hastily pushed into the dirt, and part of the handle was still visible. I left it where we found it. You guys can now take over and I'll get back to work. "I'm afraid we left some footprints."

"Miss Lee, can I see you home?"

"Just to make sure we go, I take it? No, but thank you. We walked in like pesky mosquitoes and we will walk out the same way."

"I've offended you, I fear."

"No. Actually I thought it was kinda cute."

The mosquitoes left.

I had the feeling of being followed. Probably Christopher Marchand didn't trust me to go straight home. I didn't look back to verify the sensation.

The story of Shell, which I hadn't told him, really IS a Story! My sister, Anna Lee, had been slightly over ten years older than me, and had left home for college when I was about seven. I never really knew her. She ran with her older friends, and I was just a kid, but I do remember her as being different from all the others.

Some of the kids called her 'flakey', but really she was just what had once been referred to as one of the 'flower children'. She was intelligent enough, and artistic, but after a few months in college, she'd run off to a commune. She wasn't lazy, either, and enjoyed working in the garden, raising vegetables and flowers, and playing with the dogs and kittens.

But that was the problem. The playing. Everything was a game, nothing was serious. She'd stayed there for some years, and at least wrote occasionally, so we knew where she was. Then one day she disappeared from there, and someone called Pops to see if she'd come home. They feared something might have happened to her, especially since one young man had disappeared on the same day.

When we next heard from her she was living in an abandoned shack on the beach about fifty miles away, with this same young man. Kevin McGivern was about ten years younger than Anna, more my age. We never met him, but from what little we heard from Anna, he was quite immature, and she felt more like his mother than his lover. She'd been happy in the little commune, but after he'd been there a few weeks, he wasn't, and she'd literally taken him away to try to give him a chance to 'find' himself.

Pops had wanted to send her money, but mother used the time-honored phrase about making her bed and laying in it. I was suspicious he sent some anyway, but possibly not. He'd never admitted it to me at least.

I've already said Anna was artistic. That's an understatement. The two of them made a living, such as it was (at least it put food on the table) by wandering the beaches early every morning and gathering up seashells, and any interesting driftwood they came across. With nothing to start with but a bottle of glue, Anna created fantastic items out of the shells, and Kevin apparently had something resembling business sense, and sold them to tourist shops.

Eventually the glue bottle was joined by a little paint, plaster and concrete, and later some small lights and wiring.

Driftwood can be cleaned and bleached, and either left that way as decorations, or stained and varnished, or added to other items. What couldn't be used, they burned for firewood. Not my idea of a way to live, but when we did see her she seemed happy and content.

They might actually have built a business out of it but for the fact that carelessness prevailed and Anna became pregnant. This eventually curtailed the early morning walks, but Kevin managed to gather enough to keep the little business afloat.

They married just in time to give Shell a legal name. The baby arrived late one evening, and by morning Anna had disappeared once again. She'd left a note saying the baby would be named Shell Lee McGivern, and I was to be the baby's guardian. She didn't think the father (Kevin) could handle it. She was right.

Kevin had reappeared the following morning, found his wife missing, and, according to the nurse, looked like a 'deer caught in the headlights' before he fled.

Social Services investigated, both on me, and on Mother and Pops, and agreed to my guardianship.

I'd done what I've always done. Called Kathryn. She came running, paid the hospital and Doctor bills, shopped for baby clothes, diapers, bottles and formula, while I took Shell home to Mother.

Some relative, I don't remember who, had a baby crib in their attic, which they brought, complete with a couple of sheets and blankets, and I gave up any thought I'd had of going to college. I'd just graduated from high school, and had no idea of what career path I wanted anyway, so I decided raising Shell WAS my career. I've never regretted it. I had no interest in teaching or secretarial work, which most girls end up doing. I'd have made a lousy nurse, and Medical school, which I'd also have had no aptitude for, would have cost too much.

I'm not saying we were poor, just ordinary middle class. An education at a state university would have been affordable, and I could have worked part time to help out. I still don't know what I'd have studied, maybe home economics. I'm happiest at home, and I absolutely love cooking. Shell never seemed to share that passion, and to this day she primarily eats out, or hires a cook.

Kathryn hadn't been much better. I was appalled at the state of her refrigerator when I'd finally moved into her apartment (before we'd purchased the house). It contained a few condiments, dates expired, and numerous old take-out boxes, the contents usually fuzzy and green. Since we didn't need any dubious penicillin, (I can't remember the white from the green fuzz), I'd spent my first day there hauling out the garbage and locating the nearest grocery store.

With that memory in mind, I got out my rolling pin. We'd have pie for supper.

Mutt was tugging persistently on his leash.

Okay, so you are probably going to see that line many times. But this time it was only to get closer to the pond and annoy the ducks. He'd made no further effort to explore the crime scene and willingly went where I wanted to go. I tossed some bread crumbs to the eager creatures. I know there are signs everywhere "Do Not Feed The Ducks", but they always seemed so happy to see me, I ignored the signs. I spent a lot of time watching for cops, or Park Management People.

"You're so busted," said a voice behind me.

Turning, guiltily, I found Officer Marchand watching.

"Sorry," I said.

His response was, "Oh, no. You're not one bit sorry. And you'll do it again."

"Yep."

"I'd like to feed them myself. Only I'm sworn to UPHOLD the law."

"I'm glad to hear it," I said. "What are you doing? Following me again?"

"What's again about it?"

"Didn't you follow me home yesterday afternoon?"

He said, "No, I didn't. Why, is somebody stalking you?"

"Probably not. Must have been my imagination, you know, that creepy feeling you get sometimes and there's nothing to it?"

"I do know the feeling, and usually there IS something to it. People's instincts are often correct," he replied. "Just when did that 'creepy feeling' catch up with you? And where?"

"The minute I left the park," I said, "I just thought you didn't trust me to go home and mind my own business."

"But you said you were going home."

"Yes, and I did."

"Well, it wasn't me, if it was anybody. Miss Lee, you send my subconscious mind a lot of strangely mixed signals, but not one of them calls you a liar. I trusted you. But if you do find you are being tailed, let somebody know immediately, will you?"

"Okay, but what are you doing here his morning, obviously 'tailing' me?"

He grinned, "Guilty as charged. Just thought you'd be here, and wanted to let you know the knife Mutt found did have the victim's blood on it."

"So it IS the murder weapon?"

"Seems so. Thought it only fair to tell you. Also warn you to keep it a secret until it's officially announced. Super said I could tell—if you'd promise. I was supposed to extract the promise first, of course, but you see, I do trust you to keep your word."

I said, "And I thank you for that. Has he been identified?"

"Yes. His wallet was still in his pocket. Of course the usual applies, 'Name withheld pending identification of next of kin.'

"And that's still a secret I have no authority to tell, although it will probably be on the evening news. Stay tuned, Miss Lee."

"I certainly will."

He turned to leave and I called after him, "At least you now know I didn't check his pockets while I waited."

"I didn't think you had. You were much to 'green' to have done so."

Once the pie was in the oven I e-mailed Shell. Our home had become computerized years ago for Shell's benefit. All the kids seemed to have them, and Pops wasn't going to have her feeling deprived or left out. And of course Kathryn had access to one at the office and at home. She'd tried to teach me a little more, but so far I wasn't doing so well. I'd even taken a couple of computer courses at a local community college. This resulted in more confusion. Now one more thing I didn't know was a RAM from a Byte. Shell's address was already on this list and was easy to access:

*"Dear Shell,*

*Things are happening so fast, I don't know where to begin …*".

But of course after I got started I couldn't stop. The events of two days poured out, along with my thoughts and feelings about it. I wanted to DO something, not just sit around and wait for news, but what was there to do? Shell probably would have known, and she and Joe would have been digging for answers.

But of course they had more resources than I had … a lot of computer-ese (I'd never mastered the internet, being lucky to just figure out e-mail) … and they had friends in law enforcement, plus attorneys, their own private investigator, etc.

At this point all I had was Mutt's nose, plus the apparent interest of Officer Christopher Marchand. As I described him to her, I considered the possibilities. Bribery with dinner occurred to me. Maybe I'd follow up on that idea. How could I find out what he liked best?

No ideas came to me. I'd just have to wing it.

I spent the afternoon pulling a few weeds, watering the potted plants, picking up the 'doggie doo' in the back yard, and making a pan of lasagna for supper. It was one of Kat's favorites, along with garlic bread, a tossed salad with lots of tomatoes in, a pot of tea, and of course, the cherry pie I'd made earlier. The first few times I'd made lasagna for her, she insisted on doing the garlic bread, and it always ended up burned.

The kitchen had soon become all mine. I hadn't seen any evidence that the stove top had ever been used for anything except boiling water for tea or instant coffee, and I'm sure the oven had never been turned on, much less the broiler. The microwave, on the other hand, was spattered with warmed up carry-outs. We didn't even bring it with us to the new house—and the new built-in one had not one fingerprint on it that belonged to Kat.

After supper we sat in the living room with one last cup of tea, and watched the news. Mutt's head was holding my foot down, as usual. The victim's identity was not given. Apparently the 'next of kin' had not been located, or at least notified.

About 8:00 the phone rang. Kat answered with her usual "Hello?" She never answered with her name, saying if the caller's voice was recognized as someone she didn't particularly want to talk to, she could just lower her voice about one octave and mumble, 'Sorry, wrong number', and hang up. Even the answering machine still had the original pre-recorded message.

After the initial greeting, all I heard was, "We'd be happy to. Thanks. What time?"

She hung up the phone and I inquired, "What are we going to be so happy to do?"

"Dinner with Richard and Norma. That, of course was Norma. She said she thought you might like a distraction to help you recover from your 'terrible' experience. What she's really saying, naturally, is 'picking your brains' for first hand knowledge, so she can tell her bridge club "We had Kathryn and Eleanor over for dinner Thursday. We thought it might get Eleanor's mind off the murder. She's the one, you know, who found the body, and, well, she's such a sensitive, fragile little soul we felt it might have a tragic affect on her emotionally. I thought if that were the case, Richard might be able to be of assistance."

"That," I said, "should get her all the attention she needs for that occasion. I can just hear it—'Poor little Eleanor, she's just' …"

Kat broke in, "a total wreck. Richard says …"

My turn "she'll need at least six months therapy …"

Kat, "or possibly a year. We'll…. provide all the support we can, although Eleanor is just not …"

Me: "Exactly our sort, don't you know?"

Kat: "I see you've come to know her well, in such a short time."

Me: "Not a short time at all. You've been giving me the low-down on Richard and Norma for as long as I've known you. Don't look so sheepish. I'm not at all offended. As a matter of fact, although I hope she never finds it out, I find Norma rather comical."

Suddenly we found ourselves laughing so hard we nearly rolled on the floor. Mutt woke up and licked Kat's face. She has never appreciated dog slobber and pushed him off. Disgruntled, he turned back to me, decided I wasn't totally off the wall yet, and went back to sleep.

Laughter is so cathartic.

Dinner with Norma was always a challenge, not that I'd done it very often, thank goodness, but I'd gone along, for Kat's sake, which of course was the only reason I was even included in the invitations. Kat went for Richard's sake. We occasionally invited both to our place, for the sake of Kat's conscience.

Before I'd come to Charlotte she would take her brother and his family out for dinner. Kat isn't a cook, but she will eat anything that's put in front of her.

I, on the other hand, had taken up gourmet cooking after Shell left for college. Pops was strictly a meat and potatoes man and didn't really appreciate much of what I started preparing, so I'd applied for and gotten a part-time job at a fancy country club, as chef, and enjoyed it tremendously. It was fun to watch a perfectly prepared plate leave the kitchen for someone who appreciated it, which their customers obviously did.

Norma, of course, had a housekeeper to prepare the meals, and I admit they were excellent—just not as good as mine. Really! I'm not just boasting.

I took particular delight now in having Kat's brother and family in for dinner, just to upstage Norma. I knew she looked down on me. At least she had until she'd discovered I was aunt to a VIP, being Shell, of course. I seemed to be in better favor now.

I didn't know how Richard viewed me, or my relationship with his sister, but then nobody ever knew how Richard viewed anything except his profession and his patients.

You could spend an entire evening with him and leave with the certain knowledge that he hadn't known you were there. He spent his time in his own little world, whether he was at home or in his office. He was a well-known Psychiatrist and his patients, I must admit, thought he was 'just the greatest', but I was satisfied not to be analyzed. I'd done enough self-analysis in the past to have gotten over it and decided to just be me.

He was seldom home, which left Norma to raise the two children. Kat gave all the credit to the series of housekeepers, none of which stayed long, but had apparently favorably influenced the kids. Norma was too busy out promoting her social life, working or volunteering for any good works that would serve to get her face in the news.

Somebody has to do it!

To give credit where it is due, she was the perfect wife for Dr. Richard Banks, having grown up as the daughter of another Psychiatrist who'd also never been there for his family. She was accustomed to it and to Norma it was Normal.

I went to inspect my wardrobe and choose something to wear for the evening. I also decided to call for an appointment and get my blonde, unruly, curly hair 'done' for a change, just to see if it would stay in place for the rest of the day.

Before starting that chore, I went to check my e-mail. One from Shell read:

*Darling Aunt Ellie,*

*I'm repeating my advice to 'stay out of it' and let the police take care of the investigation. And please find another place to walk the dog and stay out of the park, at least for a while. It does seem to hold true that some criminals return to the scene of their crime, and this guy (or gal as the case may be) might come back, possibly to retrieve or better dispose of the weapon, which apparently wasn't very well hidden, and it hasn't been announced as having been located.*

*Be careful dear and if you are frightened let me know and Joe and I, or just Leeanna and I, will come stay with you for a few weeks.*

*Love, Shelly*

Shelly was what most people had always called her, and she often signed off that way. But her advice was too late.

Mutt and I had already had our early morning tour around the duck pond, and I hadn't seen anything, or anyone, suspicious.

And I watched—primarily because I didn't want anyone to catch me feeding the ducks, especially Chris, who I noticed was still patrolling frequently around the park.

After unloading my bread crumbs, and onloading doggie doo into my baggies and offloading them into the trash can, I really didn't pay further attention to who might be watching.

On the walk home, Mutt was tugging persistently on his leash. I know, I'm repeating myself, but he's always anxious to walk, but equally anxious to get home and get his treats. He does love chewy doggie bones!

And I'm beginning to think I'll have to either take Shell up on having Joe come, or I'll need to haul Mutt out to the ranch for some training by Joe.

I've been able to teach him to 'sit', and the neighbor's eight-year old son has gotten him to lay down and roll over for the sake of a treat, but the word 'heel' just isn't in the pup's limited vocabulary.

Out of deference to my new hairdo, Kat drove with the top up. Usually it was down.

"Are either of the kids coming?" I asked.

"Deanna said she'd make it if she could. Daniel declined, on account of their new baby. His wife is still unwilling to leave her precious son with a sitter, and taking him along would upset Norma's applecart for the entire evening. The noisy kid would have to be stowed away somewhere out of sight and hearing, and of course that's not feasible. Personally I suspect they'd use any half-way plausible excuse."

"So there's just the five of us? Just curious, but doesn't Norma usually have BIG parties? We don't have to expect the Mayor, City Council and a couple of Senators?"

"Not tonight. She's probably afraid some of them would begin asking you questions about your murder."

"Thereby attracting attention away from her noble deeds?" I asked.

"Or simply having to recognize you as what you are, a very pretty and interesting person."

"Gosh, thanks, babe," I replied. "I feel guilty talking about her that way, but I guess I'm prejudiced due to the way she's always treated you, just as though you didn't exist."

"I know, honey. I should never have unloaded my feelings about Norma and Richard onto you. You should have had the opportunity to meet them on equal ground with no pre-judging. I may be unfair to both of them."

"At least their kids turned out okay, so something went right."

Daniel is also "Dr." Banks, but is an oncologist. He's lost his beloved grandmother to cancer many years ago, and to this day insists that's what motivated him to go in that direction. Deeanna, two years his junior, merely says he's one of those people who considers it his duty to save the world, even those smokers who don't ask to be saved. He and his wife, Alma, have two children, the youngest only three weeks old.

Deeanna had also gone her own direction, ignoring her parents' plans for her to become a nurse. She's a physical therapist instead, working for a group of orthopedic surgeons, loves her job, has no boy friends that we know of, and of course Norma would have told us unless the poor boy was totally unacceptable.

The housekeeper being busy in the kitchen, our hostess was forced to answer the door herself. "Can the sarcasm, Ellie," I mentally chastised myself. We were greeted cordially enough. Richard actually took a few seconds to look up and nod before retreating once again behind his evening newspaper. He preferred reading it for himself to getting it from the large screen TV.

Deeanna arrived shortly after we did. "Sorry, Mom, am I late? I just stopped off for a few minutes to check on a patient. Dear old gal says moving the new knee hurts, so her daughter sympathizes and won't insist. I get away with using the old saying, "No Pain, No Gain" and get her up and going. Actually she's doing quite well for her 90 years."

We were almost through dinner, everybody tactfully staying away from asking about the man in the park, when the next axe fell!

Norma was forced to answer the doorbell again.

I heard her exclaim, "Oh, No!" and she sounded so distressed I jumped up, my usual impetuous reaction, and rushed out to see what was wrong.

Two vehicles were parked out front. Four individuals hovered at the door.

One vehicle was a police car. The other had a sign on the side which indicated it was from the local animal shelter.

Two of the individuals wore police uniforms. The other two were obviously from the shelter, and one held a net, the other a strong-looking leash.

"Oh, No!" Norma repeated.

"What's wrong?" I asked.

The larger of the two policemen said, "We're here to pick up the dog."

"Why?"

"We had a complaint that he killed a toy poodle and is dangerous."

Norma still couldn't utter anything but "Oh, No." but now was adding a considerable amount of hand-wringing to it.

I said, "King Charles III? Impossible. He's gentle as a lamb. Besides, I firmly believe he couldn't get out of the yard. It's totally fenced in, and he could neither jump it nor dig under. The driveway gate is always closed. Who ordered this?"

"Lady reported to the police, we got a Court Order to pick up the dog."

By now Richard, Kat and Deeanna were all lined up behind me, and from the sound of the kitchen door, I knew the housekeeper was ready to join the fray.

"What judge?"

"Judge Anthony Essex," he replied, waving a paper at us.

"I don't believe it," I exclaimed as indignantly as I could, drawing myself up to at least five foot six inches (three of those inches were the heels of my new shoes).

"Well," said the animal control officer holding the leash, "We are required to believe it. Please produce the animal."

Deeanna by now was crying, Norma still hang-wringing, Kat and Richard stunned and unbelieving, but Deeanna went in search of King Charlie the third.

I was still ready to fight for him, "What proof is there that he's the guilty pooch?"

"All we know, ma'am is that the poodle's owner filed the complaint and we had to bother the Judge at supper to get the Order."

"Well," I said sternly, "Tony will just get disturbed again."

I dug my cell phone from the little silver purse whose strap I'd slung over my shoulder before leaving home. It was just large enough for lipstick, handkerchief (Yes, I still use fancy ones, not tissues), cell phone, and keys if necessary.

Flipping it open to my address list, I began scrolling down. "Darn," I muttered, "I don't remember if I put him under Essex, Anthony, or Tony."

"You know the Judge?" asked Richard in amazement.

"Oh, here it is, under T," I replied. "I'll explain all this to him and see what he advises."

The policeman said, "Hold up a minute lady. You got any ideas of your own? You seem…."

"Opinionated I believe is the word you're thinking and reluctant to say. Yes, I do have another idea. You get a cast of the bites on the poodle, and we take Charlie here to our vet and get casts made of his teeth. If he's guilty that will be YOUR proof. If he's not, he gets his sentence reduced to whatever time it takes to get the comparisons done. He can stay with the Vet until then, and we'll pay the boarding bill and tests.

They apparently were reluctant to bother the Judge twice in one evening about a doggie disaster. Another murdered person would have been different. One of them made a phone call, back to the police station, and finally said, "Okay. We'll do that."

"Do What?"

"What you suggest, Miss…."

"Lee," I responded, "Miss Eleanor Lee. What did they say?"

"They'll order tests on the poodle's bites, but we have to take your dog to the clinic and make sure he stays there until the casts are compared."

Deeanna had returned with King Charles III.

"See?" I said, "Gentle as can be. He's a greyhound, not a pit bull or rottweiler."

He took the leash and turned away toward his vehicle.

"Hey there, my choice of clinic. And you aren't going without me." I said, adamantly.

"Lady, you are becoming somewhat of a nuisance."

"I know. It's intentional. We take him to Lake Shore Animal Hospital, and you can either bring me back here after we drop him off, or Kathryn can come get me." I put my unused cell phone back in my purse and we left, me saying,

"Hold dessert, Norma, I'll be back." I actually wanted to hug her, but didn't quite have the nerve.

Three days later I collected Norma and we picked up her dog.

Lake Shore Animal Hospital was where we'd been taking Mutt, and we'd liked all the veterinarians and assistants there.

There seems to be no logical reason for the name of the place. I'd said so once and been told the original clinic actually was near a lake, but they'd outgrown the facility and had to build a larger hospital and move.

This left us wondering what dog had actually attacked the poor little poodle, and why the owner had so definitively identified King Charles III.

Was it a pure and simple mistake, or did somebody have a grudge against Richard, or Norma?

Anyway, as the saying goes, "All's well that ends well."

And this had, at least for Charlie the third and his owners.

But I wasn't sure what it portended for me.

Norma had suddenly become my new best friend!

Kat had said she'd be late for dinner, so I hadn't started it yet. She was wanting to stop and inspect the condition of a new listing. Some repairs and updates were being added and she wanted to be certain they'd been completed before taking a prospective buyer in to see it.

Richard, Norma and Deeanna arrived at the door a few minutes ahead of Kat. I of course invited them in and offered coffee.

"Kathryn," I said (these formal people were 'Richard, never Dick', 'Kathryn, never Kat', 'Deeanna, never Dee', 'Daniel, never Dan or Danny', and of course I was either Miss Lee or Eleanor, whatever they felt like at the moment) "isn't home yet, but should be in a few minutes if you'd care to wait."

They did. I had the distinct feeling that there was a specific purpose to the visit but had no intention of asking. These were not people who just dropped in!

Kathryn saved me by appearing almost on their heels.

I'd heard the car arrive, and the irrelevant thought crossed my mind that we were about to have a parking problem, since Richard had parked directly behind Kat's garage door. She probably left hers in the driveway behind mine, so they could leave whenever they were ready.

"We have guests," I told her at the door.

"I know. I recognized Richard's car. Deeanna's too. Did they come separately? We are going to need more parking if my entire family decides to socialize."

Since all three had arrived at one time, I hadn't noticed the extra vehicle. "Are we also expecting Daniel, Alma, Daniel, Jr. and baby Marilee?"

"I sincerely hope not. I wasn't aware of anybody at all coming."

"Got any more relatives that I don't know about?"

"None that would just show up unannounced. What does Norma want?"

We both assumed it had been Norma who had instigated the visit. "I didn't ask," was all I replied.

We joined the visitors in the living room and Kat sat down. I stayed up, saying, "Can you join us for dinner? I haven't started it yet, but we'd be happy to have you."

Richard instantly stood up, saying, "We wouldn't want to be a bother. Norma just wanted to know...."

Now we knew for sure who was steering this caravan, but I said, "if we have any news about the murder? As a matter of fact I do, but it's not a lot. Please stay. It's really no bother. You can visit while I check out the refrigerator."

Kathryn to the rescue again, "If Eleanor says it's okay, then it IS! She's always prepared, like a good Girl Scout."

Richard, after a significant glance from his wife, sat down again, "That would be very nice, Eleanor. Thanks."

Cooking for Norma would have to be at least somewhat gourmet. I'd been planning to use up some leftovers. Having lived frugally all my life, it seemed a waste to throw out good, edible food.

Frankly, that made it easy. I opened a few cans at random, dumped out the contents, along with anything I found in the refrigerator, started heating it up, and started making a pile of crepes. A good mushroom sauce on top, a salad, and the dessert I'd already made would have to suffice.

Deeanna came bouncing into the kitchen, as much as she'd allow herself to bounce, with her mother in the room just behind her, saying, "Can I help?"

I pointed to the cupboard, "You can set the table. Dishes in that cabinet, silverware in the drawer below. Napkins to the right", and reached for the coffee pot. "French vanilla or butternut?" I asked.

"Huh?"

"Coffee flavor."

"Oh. Doesn't matter. Butternut, I guess."

"Do we need cream and sugar?"

"I think we all drink it black, but I'll ask before I do the table."

She was reaching for plates. I stopped her. "Probably best to fix the plates here—just take the silverware and napkins, salt, pepper, etc."

"Okay."

I was breaking up lettuce, cutting peppers, tomatoes and black olives when she returned. "Any favorites on salad dressing? If not you all just get my house special."

She reported that we didn't need cream but sugar would be appreciated, and was standing at the cupboard with her back to the door, reaching for the sugar bowl, when the kitchen door opened again.

Assuming (which one should never do) that it was Kat, I said, "Would you just light the candles?" Anything to keep Kat's fingers out of the cooking.

A male voice answered, "Sure. Got a match or lighter? I don't smoke."

There was a crash behind me as Deeanna dropped the sugar bowl. "Chris?"

"Deeanna?"

Exit time, I thought. Escape Plan: "Deeanna, don't step in it."

The bowl hadn't broken, but there was sugar everywhere. "I'll go find the dust buster. I think I left it in the garage."

I escaped.

I took my time locating the dust buster, and when I returned to the kitchen, Chris and Deeanna were behaving like casual acquaintances, an impression I'd not originally gotten.

We persuaded Chris to join us for dinner and Deeanna set another place.

I made three more crepes and dumped another can into the pot.

We decided to put the salad plates on, with a large salad bowl, and let people help themselves. A plate of warm croissants and dish of honey-butter went on with it, for anybody who could use the extra starch. Personally I thought the crepes didn't call for anything more, but you never know about hungry men.

Six at the table meant I wouldn't have my left-over pie for late snack, but NEVER would I cut a pie in seven or eight pieces, just for the sake of having a piece left. Pie, in my opinion, was meant to be cut in SIX only. Anything else was cheating the guest. I don't really care if you already weigh four hundred pounds. That's YOUR problem, and you can always refuse dessert. Not that you would if you weighed that much. More likely have seconds.

I filled the crepes, rolled them, drizzled on the sauce. A couple of slices of spiced apples and sprig of mint and the plates were ready for the table.

Norma's reaction was "This is delicious, Eleanor. I don't know how you did it in such a short time."

Nobody else commented. Too busy eating!

"It's really a very simple recipe," I replied. "Takes no time at all. And dessert was already made."

Kat, pardon me, Kathryn asked, "And dessert consists of…."

"I'm not telling. Wait and see."

More compliments were forthcoming when I produced the no-bake lime cheesecake with kiwi garnish.

Norma wanted the recipe.

Deeanna, having suddenly decided I was her aunt, exclaimed, "Yes, Aunt Ellie, this is heavenly. How did you make it?"

"Not much secret to it. I cheated. Used a graham cracker crust from the store, mixed up that old cream cheese and whipped topping recipe using a packet of lime gelatin instead of the sugar. The kiwi is just a color match, besides which I really like it. You could use any flavor gelatin you wanted, and any topping. I've done the same thing mixing in shaved chocolate, or chopped nuts, then topping with the same added ingredient. It has limitless possibilities, and only takes a few minutes to make."

We retired to the living room with our coffee, or wine for anyone who wanted it, and I asked, "Did you have a purpose in coming over, Chris dear, or were you just hoping for dessert?"

"Both, it seems," he said, "Actually I wanted to tell you that the murder victim's family has finally been found and notified, and disclosure will be on the evening news."

"Which is coming on any minute," I said. "Anybody who sees the remote, please turn it on."

Richard did, having found it by his chair (the one Kat usually sits in).

Deeanna sat down, then got up again, "I think we've got just enough time to clear the table, Aunt Ellie."

Chris decided to help.

During a break when Deeanna was in the dining room and Chris and I were in the Kitchen, out of her hearing, I whispered "She's the one? I mean the 'maybe' girl friend you mentioned?"

"It's obvious, I guess. Yes. Is this evening possibly going to be an ice breaker for me?"

"Yep," I said. "Sure is."

I'd asked him during one of our short walks in the park if he had a girl, and he'd replied that he 'sort of' did, but wasn't sure that just a cop would be acceptable in the eyes of her highbrow family.

Now I said, "Remember what I said. You have completed college, gotten a degree in law enforcement. You are intelligent, handsome, young, and have nowhere to go but up!"

"Yes, ma'am, I'll remember."

"If there's one thing I've learned in my forty-five years, it's to believe what wiser minds have come up with: 'All men, and I'll add women, are created equal.'"

He grinned, "Seems like I've heard that somewhere."

"And from Pop, Kat and Shell, I've also learned to back down from no-one. A person is just as good as he thinks he is. Self-esteem comes from within, and I'll take no guff from you about being just a cop.

"One small piece of advice, however. Until you feel totally accepted by any group, or family, stay away from two subjects: politics and religion."

"Sounds like a good policy."

"And I'll do my part. I may be vertically challenged, my niece still towers over me by a good three inches even when I'm wearing my high heels, but I'm not exactly without influence in this family."

"Little but mighty," he said.

"Just call me Mighty Mouse."

Deeanna came back into the kitchen, caught me kissing Chris on the cheek and said, "Hey, Aunt Ellie, keep your mitts off. He's mine."

I winked at him, gave him a thumbs up, and we all returned to the living room to see what the TV anchor was going to report.

I already knew.

*"Dear Shell, (and Joe of course)*

*"I've had a very strange, interesting, and sometimes confusing day. It's a little after midnight and as usual I feel the need to unload on you...."*

At last everyone had gone. Kat was already asleep and I disturbed Mutt when I pulled my foot from under his head.

He woke up sufficiently to follow me to the kitchen, possibly thinking of leftovers, but finding only dog kibbles in his dish, went to his bed and promptly went back to sleep. I knew he'd follow me upstairs and try to sleep on my bed when I eventually got there.

I'd booted up my computer, which I keep in the corner of the kitchen. Kat uses one spare bedroom as a home office, but I'd chosen this corner for mine. I didn't need much space. But this was convenient to keep recipes, write letters, e-mail friends and relatives, keep household accounts, etc., while still hearing the timer telling me to check the oven to see if the cake was done.

I considered it much too late to telephone Shell, especially since the advent of a baby in the house results in a considerable loss of sleep all by itself. No need for unnecessary phone calls from aunts in distress.

So I told her the story of my day:

As previously stated, I already knew what the TV newsman was going to say, so it was no surprise to hear the pretty girl announce all the things they were going to report on, then the middle-aged chief anchor chimed in with "We've been advised of the identity of the man found dead in the park...."

They'd 'finally located' next of kin, the gentleman's wife, who had been visiting with friends out of town.

I knew she'd been 'hiding out', not just visiting.

Fortunately, they'd withheld my name, and Mutt's, saying only that he'd been found by a 'lady walking her dog in the park', and I knew I had Chris and the police chief, as well as my friend, the judge, to thank for that.

We'd gone extra early to the park in the morning, and for once, Mutt was NOT tugging persistently on his leash, but had at last decided to 'heel', so maybe I wouldn't have to resort to getting him professionally trained after all. He was a really intelligent creature and I was beginning to have some hope for his manners.

Why go early? Because I knew I'd catch up with the Judge!

We'd found Tony on the far side of the pond, he sitting on a bench as though waiting for us. His dog seemed happy to see us too. It gave both him and Mutt somebody to sniff who didn't audibly object.

"I thought you'd be here," Tony said.

"Got any news?" I asked.

"Yes, and it will be on the evening news if you want to turn it on. Please don't tell anything I disclose before that, will you?"

"If you say it's confidential, then it is."

"The victim is George Gianelli, owner and operator of the restaurant of the same name," said the Judge. "If we are to believe what we've been told so far, he and his wife, Eva, had a big blow-up and she got in her Porsche and drove to Atlanta to stay with a friend."

"Male?"

"It would appear so, yes."

"Was this friend the cause of the blow-up?"

"Apparently not. The usual fights are over either infidelity or money. This one appears to have been over not getting enough of the green stuff.

"Anyway, she was located and brought back as a 'person of interest' but not arrested. The family attorney actually got to the Court House before she did. It's a long ride from Atlanta, and she'd called ahead.

"According to her story, she'd already left town early Tuesday morning, and naturally the friend verifies her story."

I said, "So it's either bust her alibi or she walks?"

"You've been reading too many detective stories, Ellie."

"Mostly 'defective' stories. I find a lot of errors, discrepancies and inconsistencies. Also a lot of plain missing details which leave gaps, things which should have been included to explain some situation or other. I find myself making up the rest in my own mind."

He said, "I know the feeling. That's the same kind of gaps lawyers and witnesses leave me and the juries to fill in for ourselves. But of course those are deliberate, meant to obfuscate and confuse, and undoubtedly the fiction is just careless oversight on the part of the author."

"Probably," I said, "I'd better get going—you too if you don't want to be late to Court."

We finished feeding the ducks and walked around to where he was parked, and said goodbye.

"For now, Ellie. Come early any time you feel the need."

And I will, of course.

This is the reason I wasn't surprised at the announcement. What did surprise me, however, was Richard's reaction to the news.

His hand shook and he spilled his coffee.

Norma jumped up, ever the good wife, to mop up with a napkin. "Did you get burned?"

"No. Sorry about the chair, Kathryn. I'm afraid I spilled on it too."

"Not to worry," she said, being ungrammatical for her, "It will wash."

"Wash?" asked Richard.

"Oh, brother dear, don't you recognize that old chair? It was Mom's and I couldn't give it up, so I had it slip-covered. They got a good job on it, didn't they?"

"Looks like upholstery," said Norma.

"Well, anyway, stop worrying about it and tell us what startled you that much."

The good Doctor didn't answer. He was, instead, staring inquiringly at me. "You knew this, didn't you, Eleanor?"

"Yes. Tony told me this morning when I met him at the park."

"Tony?"

It was Chris who answered, "Judge Anthony Essex. He asked me to come over and fill in any details the newspeople didn't cover."

"Which is?" I asked.

"Not much. They seem to have it all." he replied.

"Except my name, for which I am thankful."

"Oh, Aunt Ellie, don't kid yourself," Chris said.

I'm now not only Norma's best friend, but everybody's aunt.

"They know it. Chief and Judge Essex stopped them from saying it. Chief said it was a safety measure, just in case the perpetrator thought you might have seen him."

"Or her," I said.

"Yeah. Or her."

Kathryn spoke up, "That doesn't explain YOUR reaction, Richard. I'm asking you to explain."

He said, "Until they said Eva had been located I was afraid she might have been killed also."

"Eva?" asked Norma.

"Been a patient of mine for seven or eight months. She missed her appointment Tuesday. At first I was just annoyed. She's done it before, then called Darlene, apologizing and asking for a new appointment. It's irritating, how irresponsible people can be. I've stayed late more than once trying to make up these lost hours. I'm just relieved to hear she's all right."

Then he added, "This is confidential, of course. Patient confidentiality, you know."

We knew.

In spite of the late night, Mutt and I went to the park early. Tony was already on his favorite bench, his rather docile dog at his feet.

We'd first met, in this very spot, during the second trip Mutt and I had made there together.

I'd been there before, of course, feeding the ducks, but usually later in the day, and no one else had been present.

He'd been sitting in the same spot, with the same dog, and had apparently walked the trail through the trees, not along the edge of the water, because....

Yes, Mutt had been persistently tugging on his leash. Nose to the ground, following some trail only he could dream of. I, of course had followed him, having not much choice. He really was a powerfully built pup, although not yet fully grown.

Which is why I'd come out of the trees unseen and was able to walk up behind him, saying, "You're SO busted!"

He'd looked up at me and replied, "Yep. I could probably be disbarred."

"Lawyer?" I said, "Well, since I may some day need one, I guess I won't report you. Especially since I'm a co-offender."

I pulled my bag of bread crumbs from my oversized purse, which I always hung over my shoulder, making me look a little lopsided, and joined him in tossing their breakfast out for the eager ducks.

"You should hang that long strap over your head, from the other shoulder. My wife says it's much more comfortable that way."

"Good idea," I said, and pulled it over my head. "You're right. Or rather I should say your wife is."

"Nice dog," he said.

"Well, I guess he will be if he ever learns some manners," I replied. "Your dog seems well-behaved. Maybe he could teach Mutt to at least heel."

"I know a good trainer if you ever need one."

"Thanks," I said, "I may have to call you."

Tony gestured to the empty side of the bench and said, "Fellow lawbreakers should stick together. Have a seat."

"So could I have your business card, just in case?"

"I don't happen to have one on me", he said, "But you can find us here most mornings."

"So where is your office located?"

"Court House," he'd replied, "I'm Judge Anthony Essex."

With Shell for my niece, Kathryn as my friend, and Paul Rayburn as my Niece's step-father, I'm not easily awed by names or titles.

I said, "I'll just call you Tony."

On this day, however, I sat down without invitation and said, "Thanks for keeping my name out of the news."

"No problem," he replied. "I figured you wouldn't appreciate the notoriety."

"You're SO right."

There was a second cappuccino on the bench. "Mine?" I asked.

"Uh huh," he said as he continued to break up his left-over donut and toss it out, along with my usual bread offering. "I knew you'd be here this morning."

Mutt, for a change, had decided to sit down beside Duchess instead of harassing the feathered friends as he usually did.

One of the things I'd learned on our second meeting had been the name of his dog, a beautiful greyhound. She greatly resembles Norma's King Charles III. But I guess I don't know one greyhound from another. I'm sure they do NOT all look alike, but if they aren't a completely mixed breed, a Labrador, a Poodle, or a Spaniel, I can't tell the difference.

He asked, "Was your evening interesting?"

"Sure was," I replied, "I discovered Chris' girl friend is Deeanna, Richard's daughter. And Richard spilled his coffee, but not over Chris. I don't think he suspects that yet."

"Then what caused the spill?"

"Eva Gianelli's name."

He took another sip of his cappuccino, threw out the remainder of his donut and asked, "And why would that be?"

And so I related the events of the previous evening, including the fact that Eva was a patient of Richard's.

"Not too surprising," was Tony's response. "The DA tells me she's a sort of a basket case. Nice professional psychiatric term, but that's what he called Mrs. Gianelli. Of course since her alibi currently holds up, she's home and free to visit the good Doc, and probably should, as soon as possible."

"Then I suppose Richard will be putting in more late evenings, since Darlene will have to squeeze out an appointment time."

"Nothing going on there is there? I mean with those late evenings?" he asked.

"I certainly wouldn't think so. Norma would somehow know, and that long string attached to his ankle would have its other end around her wrist."

Tony said, "Sounds like you are getting along better with Norma."

"Don't get sarcastic," I responded. "However, I do hope to, for the sake of Kathryn, Chris, and Deeanna."

"Time to go to work," he said, "See you tomorrow?"

"Maybe."

I would, of course.

I did. Mutt was alternately tugging and heeling, whichever mood took him. He was anxious to see his pal, Duchess. I was anxious to see Tony.

Don't get me wrong. There's nothing going on between Tony and me, although he'd once joked, "If we weren't both otherwise committed, Ellie, I'd probably hit on you."

We both knew what he meant. We each really liked the other and he's probably the only man since Pop died that I was entirely comfortable with. We could, and did, talk about anything and everything that was on our minds, knowing that anything said would be both understood, and completely confidential.

He'd said pretty much the same thing, "There are few people I can be just 'me' with. The rest of the time I have to behave like a Judge. Believe me, Ellie, I like the job, but I consider it to be somewhat like the Doctor, or the Priest, Rabbi, or Minister. There often is, and should NOT be, any evidence of immorality or impropriety seen in anyone the people are supposed to be able to trust completely. At heart I guess I'm sort of impish, and decorum isn't always easy to maintain."

Today we took the direct route, following the shoreline. Tony smiled. Duchess barked. Mutt tugged. I was forced to hurry or be dragged.

Since I was in a real hurry this morning anyway, I had no objection to the dragging.

I plopped myself down on the bench beside Tony. Mutt plopped himself down beside Duchess and began drooling all over her. Better her than me, I thought. I was already dressed for the day and wouldn't have time to change.

"Okay, girl," said Tony, always sensitive to people's moods and feelings, "Just what have you been up to?"

At age forty-five it's really neat to be called girl. I wasn't sure how much I wanted to say, and remained silent for a moment.

"Something finally worrying you?" he asked.

"No. Yes. I guess so."

"What?" he demanded to know.

"Well, nothing was scary until I came across the Rykers."

Now he was really serious, "And just what do you know about the Rykers, and how did you 'come across' them?"

"I didn't. Not really. I guess, well, I guess I said too much to Shell."

"Your niece?"

"Yeah. You see, I tried to find some information on Gianelli, and I'm sort of an internet dud. I couldn't find much outside of white and yellow pages data on address, phone numbers, you know the kind of thing. Home address, business address of the restaurant." I stopped.

"So you talked to Shell."

"Yes. And she sort of—well—ummm—she sicced her PI onto it, and he found them."

Tony said, "Your niece has a Private Investigator? How come?"

"On permanent retainer. His name is Patrick Abrams. Abe has other business, but when Shell calls everything else gets dropped, or at least she gets preferential treatment."

"And this Abe fellow discovered?"

"He couldn't find anything detrimental to say about Gianelli, except that he'd married Eva Ryker."

"Uh, huh. Go on."

"I'm beginning to suspect you already know. The Ryker family has a totally clean record, except that people they have problems with develop bigger problems. Everyone always has an airtight alibi however."

"Uh, huh," he said again. "Now I suggest you tell me why Shell has a PI on permanent retainer."

"It's a long story," I replied, "And I haven't got time right now."

"Why?"

"I have to get to the airport."

"Leaving town?" he asked, "Running for safety?"

"No. Just picking up Moira."

"Moira who?"

"Moira Abrams. Part of Abrams Investigations. She's coming to visit for a while."

He asked, "Personal bodyguard? Guardian Angel? What?"

"Both, I guess. Shell insists on sending her. She's a former police detective who works for her son since she retired."

"I'll take you to the airport. We can drop Mutt and Duchess off in your back yard. What flight is Moira coming in on?"

"None of them." I said. "Well, that's not literally true. Just not by airline. Julie is bringing her."

"Julie? More people I don't know about?"

"Pilot of Shell's two planes. Well, actually, one of them is a helicopter, but of course that's not for long flights. They use it mostly for short hops, from accidents to the hospital, rescue work, that kind of thing."

"Now I know I'm taking you to the airport. You are going to spend the time filling me in on the apparently strange life of your niece."

"Just remember I warned you. It's not a short story."

We dropped Duchess and Mutt off in the fenced back yard.

And headed for the airport.

Shell's story, of course, begins when my older sister sneaked out of the hospital, leaving only a note with my name and telephone number on it. But Tony knows all that.

In spite of having no mother and father, her life was pretty ordinary. She had me, a substitute mother, although from the beginning I called myself 'Aunt Ellie'. I never let her think I was her mother. And she had grandparents, Mother and Pops.

In the beginning mother had been a tremendous help. When it came to raising babies, what I knew could fly into your eye on the wing of a gnat and you'd never have felt it. Kat had a nephew and niece, but since Richard's marriage to Norma, they had never been close. She did have a real talent for shopping however, and had outfitted Shell quickly and efficiently, no doubt with the assistance of the sales clerk.

Mother had died when Shell was about nine years old, but since her health had deteriorated for several years she hadn't been much help. Life went on as usual, only instead of four people and a cat in the house there were now three people and the cat. His name was Spook, so called because he had a talent for disappearing. Spook had more hiding places than a regular outdoor dog has fleas. His other chief talent was knowing when he was due for a trip to the Vet for his shots. It sometimes took hours to find and catch him.

Tony, by now, also knew all of that. What he didn't know was how life changed one day after Shell had graduated and taken a job as policewoman in our hometown.

He didn't know about how Anna, (now Paul Rayburn's widow) when she knew she was dying, had sent Investigator Alan Carstens to get Shell and persuade her to come to Wyoming.

Initially Shell thought Paul had been just a busy, hard-working rancher, and when Anna died she was stunned to learn from her attorney the extent of her inheritance.

She had flown by commercial airline with Alan. They hadn't wanted her at that time to discover she could have come by private jet. Anna had wanted her daughter to see her as a simple housewife, not as the widow of a billionaire.

They had preferred Shell to grow up with the same simple values they had, while making certain she had everything she needed, made sure she wasn't spoiled. Life on the ranch was, while comfortable, not lavish.

When her life had been threatened, her former boss, Police Chief Joe Sheppard, had resigned and run to the rescue, just in time to save her from being murdered by her housekeeper and Alan Carstens.

I gave Tony an abbreviated version as he drove me to the airport.

We arrived just in time to watch Shell's big silver bird touch down and taxi in. I immediately noticed the new addition on the plane's nose. Shell had promised the Ryan family she'd do something to honor Erin, and had painted a discreet dark green shamrock on the nose of the jet, with the single word 'Erin' under it. It definitely added character to the big plane. I'm betting it gets lots of comments as well as questions.

Tony was impressed. "I didn't expect anything quite that large," he said.

"Well," I replied, "It's not a 747, but Shell and Joe made a recent trip to Ireland, taking along Leeanna, Moira, a couple of guests, and two pilots, of course, and had space left over for quite a few more. It's outfitted with a couple of rather large rest rooms, several bunk beds, tables, big chairs and couches, not regulation aircraft seating. Would you like a quick tour, that is if Julie has time for a short layover?"

He did. And Julie did, having to take time to refuel and check to make certain her return flight plans had been duly noted at the airport.

If Tony was impressed by the jet, Moira was equally impressed by what she referred to as "my" Judge. I told her not only was he NOT mine, but he was already taken. She facetiously responded that she didn't need him anyway, at least not yet.

"Expecting to get into trouble while you are here?" he asked.

"I sincerely hope not," she replied. "But nothing is guaranteed."

I asked Julie if she could stay over, have dinner with us and leave tomorrow.

"I'll have to check with Shell. And Bob, of course." Bob is her husband.

Having done that, she of course had to change her flight plans, but at last we were headed home.

On the drive, Moira and Julie filled us in on more details of the recent trip to Ireland, and showed off their 'souvenir' jewelry.

"Shell sent some for you and Kathryn, too. We hope you like it," said Julie.

Now of course I had to change my dinner plans to include Julie—but that wasn't much of a problem, as I'd already planned extra for Moira and could just add another potato to the pan.

But first I checked my e-mail. There was one from Shell which read:

*Dear Aunt Ellie,*

*I hope you like Moira as much as we do. She's really a special person and I'll feel much better knowing she's with you. We considered sending Joe's dog, Mitch, along as well, but Moira doesn't know all the correct commands, and he might not get along with Mutt. Knowing your love for your pooch, it didn't seem like a good idea to take the chance.*

*Leeanna is growing so fast, crawling everywhere and already trying to pull herself up to walk. No piece of furniture or low hanging drapery is safe from her. Dad says she's worse than any two small kittens. He should know. His wife Jessie just got two little ones from the Shelter and he comments that in addition to curtains and furniture they try to climb his pant legs. I know the feeling, remembering when Lucky was that small!*

*Take care!*

*We love you.*

*Shell, Joe, Mac, Jessie, Leeanna, Mitch and Lucky*

I wrote back:

*Dear Shell,*

*Moira is charming and I'm certain we will enjoy her visit.*

*Glad you DID NOT send Mitch. We might have had open warfare. I have no idea what Mutt might do if anyone did attack me. He's still so playful, and also friendly, he'd probably just lick them to death, thinking it was a game.*

*I really don't see any danger to me. I didn't see anybody, or hear anything. The fellow was beyond help when Mutt found him, and I'm told he'd been dead for a short time already, but since everybody else seems concerned, I'll be happy to include Moira in our morning walks.*

*And don't worry about space—we have a couple of extra rooms. Come visit some time soon and you'll see what we've done with the place. Mutt is finally learning that he's not to dig up my plants and bushes, thank goodness.*

*Love, Aunt Ellie*

The following morning we got up to a dreary, dark sky and imminent storm warnings and decided it was a good time to take another cup of cappuccino out to the back porch and just relax. Even Kat stayed for a short time, finally leaving for the office about mid-morning.

"Nice," was Moira's comment, "owning your own business. But I don't suppose that entitles you to much time off."

"Right. Actually it makes it more imperative to be on the job early and stay late," was Kat's response. "None of my staff goof off much, probably because I don't give them the opportunity. But that leaves Ellie and I less time to spend doing other things."

"Such as?"

"Oh, dinners out, golf, theater … that kind of thing."

Moira perked right up. "You two golf? I love it. Wyoming weather cuts the season short, however. Where do you play? Maybe Ellie and I can go out some time," she said. Then in dismay, "Oh, shucks, my clubs are in Cheyenne."

"You can use mine," said Kathryn. "Ellie knows where they are. They don't get much use, and you are quite welcome."

"Thanks. I might just do that. But unless the weather clears, it won't be today."

It wasn't! Even Mutt didn't want to stay out and play in the rain, preferring to sprawl on his bed and sleep through it.

Having nothing much else to do, I decided to catch up on my baking. Moira helped for a while, then curled up with a book she found on my 'mystery' shelf.

A gal after my own tastes at last. Kat would rather spend the entire day reading every word in the Wall Street Journal! How boring!

Next morning dawned bright and clear and soon found the three of us, Me, Tony and Moira, squeezed onto the single bench at the far side of the pond.

Mutt and Duchess had decided to irritate the ducks.

The ducks were blissfully ignoring them in favor of eating the stale cake I'd brought and Tony's left-over donuts.

"Tony," I said, "It's time somebody took over your dietary habits. You should at least bring oat bran muffins, or bagels. All those donuts can't be good for your cholesterol."

"You keep your hands off my so-called dietary habits, girl," he replied. "Some of the things you've been doing are more dangerous to your health than my donuts are to mine."

I asked what he meant and he said, "Continuing your sleuthing."

"Why? What are you talking about, Tony?"

"Attending Gianelli's visitation. Do you think that was a wise move?"

"How did you find out I did that?" I inquired.

He said, "Oh, I have my spies."

"Apparently."

"Well? Are you going to explain yourself?"

"It seems I must."

I hate stories that backtrack. I also hate stories that add recipes, gardening ideas and dog grooming tips just in order to add pages to the book. I like my stories straight up and simple, but here goes:

BACKTRACKING:

Eva Gianelli had made funeral plans for her husband, and as soon as the medical examiner released his body, the mortuary put them in motion.

I had no intention of attending services, but decided I would go to the visitation, which was from 4 to 8 p.m. the day preceding the funeral.

I had no reason to. I hadn't known the man, or ever met the widow.

Okay, so I was curious. Shell would have said snooping. I hadn't told her of my intention, as I'm certain she'd have tried to forbid it. I don't take orders well, but don't like receiving them either, so avoiding them seems a viable option.

I arrived early, knowing that there would be a large crowd for a man so well known. After all, he had all those fancy restaurants, and had made a habit of wandering around talking to the customers. Everybody had known him, and the circumstances of his death would bring out the curiosity seekers who hadn't.

It turned out to be a good decision. Only one person was there when I arrived, and she was just turning to leave.

I approached the beautiful woman wearing traditional black, including hat and veil, and extended my hand.

"Do I know you?" she asked.

"No, but I wanted to offer my sympathy anyway, and any assistance that might be of help to you." I said.

"I haven't been in Charlotte very long, but I have been in your restaurant. My reason for coming are that my dog and I were the ones who found your husband in the park. I can't help feeling that if we'd been just a little earlier, it might not have happened. Just our presence there might have deterred whoever killed him. Or if we'd been a little earlier perhaps we could have saved him. I don't know why, but there's just a feeling of guilt creeping up on me every time I think about it."

She wiped away an invisible tear (being hidden by the veil) and said, "Oh, my dear, you mustn't blame yourself. You probably couldn't have done anything, and possibly even endangered yourself, maybe been killed too."

Odd, but I hadn't thought of that.

A young girl appeared from behind a sofa. I hadn't noticed her until she followed me to the door. She seemed to be much in distress.

I held out my hands. I had the impression that she wanted to say something—then changed her mind and only said, "Thank you for coming" before quickly turning away.

Tony stood up, called the obedient Duchess, connected the leash to her collar, then turned to look at Moira.

She rewarded him with a little crooked smile. She knew exactly what he was thinking. I was afraid I did too.

The friend had suddenly disappeared as he turned his attention to me. Only the Judge remained as he said:

"Not so long ago I was a trial lawyer, Eleanor."

The 'Eleanor' instead of the usual friendly 'Ellie' was a trifle intimidating, although he hadn't said it harshly.

He continued, "And I haven't lost any of my interrogation skills."

I said, "And what's that supposed to mean?"

"It means you haven't said everything. I know it. Moira knows it. And YOU know it. What you have NOT said was WHY you went. I think I know, but you are going to tell us before I leave this spot!"

I glanced appealingly at Moira, but she only nodded and said, "Ellie, you said she was beautiful. How could you tell, with all that black, and the veil and all?"

Annoyed, I replied, "I said the dress was black. Did I forget to mention that it fit exceedingly well?"

"Oh, okay, I guess. But how about the veil?"

"It wasn't so heavy as to disguise the perfect features. Only just enough to louse up any good eye contact."

The Judge asked, "And that's really why you went, wasn't it? To look the poor widow square in the eye and size her up?"

I was still annoyed. "The wealthy widow, I think would be correct."

"Fine," said the Judge. "I'll concede that she can live more than comfortably for the rest of her life, if you will just concede that I was right?"

"Okay," I said, "Pops taught me at an early age to always look people in the eye when talking to them. He said the mouth can lie, often quite convincingly, but the eyes will give you away. They really are the mirror to the soul, you know."

Moira said "And you were thwarted by the veil."

"Yes."

Tony was back. Pushing one of my recalcitrant curls back and looking me straight in the eyes, he said, "I believe you, Ellie. But promise me you'll stop sleuthing."

"No. I can't. I don't know exactly why, but I can't do that."

"Then be careful."

With a little salute to Moira and a small hand gesture to Mutt to not follow, he left.

I wondered if he talked Mutt's language.

I'd have to ask.

We woke up to another rainy day. After letting the dog out into the back yard, the three of us sat down to breakfast.

Moira said, "No park run today. How about a shopping trip? I promised my grandkids I'd bring back something from North Carolina."

"Do that," said Kathryn, "and meet me for lunch somewhere. Just don't go shoe shopping without me. That's MY day." She gathered up her purse and briefcase and prepared to leave for work. As usual I had to locate her keys.

When she'd gone, Moira asked, "What's that about the shoes? Sounds like a story."

"You figured that out fast," I said.

"Used your eye watching tip," was her reply.

I said, "Okay, but I warn you it's a boring story."

I'd first met Kathryn in front of a shoe store in Charlotte.

I'd spent the summer with a grandmother in the city, and it was the day before I was to return home to begin the next school session.

Mom had sent me some money, and grandma had given me a little more, and I was told I could shop for my own school clothes. I'd thought I could do that a long time ago. After all, I was sixteen, but mother had always gone along to make sure I didn't get anything she considered inappropriate, or extravagant.

I'd gotten a few things, and had some money left. Not a lot. Not enough to buy the shoes in that window. I really wanted them. All the kids had them. Mother would have said they cost too much, but I was practically drooling on the sidewalk I wanted them so bad.

Staring in the window, knowing I didn't dare walk through the door, I hadn't noticed when she came to stand beside me.

"Hi, girl," she said, "I take it you are out school shopping."

"Yeah," I replied, "I have to go home tomorrow so this is my last chance, at least in the City. My home town doesn't have stuff like this."

"So are you going to try some on?"

"I guess not. The ones I want are too expensive, and even if I did have enough money left, mother would make me take them back."

She put her arm around my shoulders and said, "How about I buy them for you? Then they'd be a gift, and you can't return a gift, you know."

"Oh, I couldn't let you do that. Mother would have a fit. Besides …" I moved away from her comforting arm … "Besides that, Pops always says…."

"That you mustn't talk to strangers. I know. My mother always used to say the same thing, and I guess I never learned to listen. How is anybody supposed to become anything other than a stranger if they don't talk to each other?"

That made me laugh.

Then she said, "Anyway, this is a VERY public street and there are lots of people in the store to protect you from me. Or me from you for that matter. Come on. I was going in to buy shoes for myself, and you might at least try them on."

We did, and to my everlasting shame, I accepted her offer. It turned out to be the best thing I'd ever done, and resulted in this lifetime friendship, and eventual partnership.

Kat did buy shoes, and I later discovered she'd purchased the cheapest pair in the place, switched the sales slip for the ones she'd gotten for me, and donated the others to the Salvation Army. She'd had no intention of shopping for shoes that day.

I asked how I was going to explain this at home, and she said to tell my mother I'd found a sale … just omit the fact that they were not 'on sale' but at least anything in the store was at least 'for sale', and I didn't need to account for them any other way.

She still has a quirky way with words, twisting them to her own satisfaction. I often tell her she should have been a con artist, and her reply is "maybe I am, honey."

Years later when I finally asked her why she stopped to talk to me that day her answer was "It broke my heart to see someone so young, lost and forlorn. You were desperate for some kindness and affection, and I had no recourse but to offer it. I'm not sorry. I will never be sorry. It brought us together."

She still doesn't know how completely right she was. But that's a story that died with Grandma, Pops and mother, and rightly so.

At least that's what I'd thought, until recently.

Now it seemed to be returning to haunt me.

Moira and I walked into Gianellli's restaurant at precisely noon. By now I was more than annoyed. I was quite royally ticked off.

My disposition isn't usually this bad, but this day had definitely not been going my way and it had all begun with our morning dog walk at the park.

Things were fine until Tony got up, put Duchess on her leash and then turned back to me, asking "Are you two free for lunch?"

I replied that I'd simply intended to fix something at home, but what did he have in mind?

He said, "Just a minute until I check."

He got out his cell phone, dialed a number and we heard him say, "Hi, sweetheart. Are you able to meet me for lunch this noon?"

Apparently 'sweetheart' was available, as he then said, "I'll give you a call when we decide where and when. I have a couple of people I'd like you to meet."

I'd automatically hauled my phone out of my pocket, saying, "I'll call Kat to see if she's available."

"No."

"What?" I asked.

"I didn't ask Kathryn. I specifically asked you and Moira. This is strictly a foursome," said Tony.

"Okay, then I'll just call and let her know we won't be home for lunch."

"And tell her later where we are going, so she can just show up? Moira, take her cell phone away from her and don't let her have it back until after lunch."

He snatched it from my hand and gave it to her. "I mean it. No calls, outgoing or incoming."

"You don't trust me?" I asked, indignantly.

"Not where Kathryn is concerned," he responded. "Your life revolves around her, and you are bound to tell her. You tell her everything! And this time you are not to. I have my reasons. Can't you please just trust me?"

"Looks like I'll have to," I said, watching Moira pocket my phone.

He didn't know it but I actually do have a few secrets known only to myself.

I saw them immediately, seated at a choice table with an attentive waiter already hovering over them. The waiter laid down two additional menus and departed.

I was still mad. But upon being introduced "Eleanor Lee, Moira Abrams, meet my darling wife, Helen," I melted under her loving eyes. After all, it was Tony I was mad at, not his innocent spouse. She had to put up with him full time. I only had a few minutes every morning, and then usually with Mutt, Duchess and Ducks as topics of conversation.

It occurred to me that God's critters are great intermediaries. They do, however, take sides, being loyal creatures. I wished Mutt was here!

We'd decided on Gianelli's at noon. I probably should have said I decided, since that was my immediate choice after Tony asked where we'd like to meet.

He shook his head, saying, "Girl, you've got to let this obsession go."

"I'm not obsessed. Well, maybe I am, just a little. But it's a great place. Kat and I have been there a few times. The food is great and I know Moira will like it."

He'd reluctantly acquiesced and here we were.

"So tell me why we are here." I demanded.

"Not until after everyone has ordered," he'd replied, pointing at the menu on the table before me.

The waiter returned, we placed our orders and I said, "NOW, please."

"I told you. I wanted you lovely ladies to meet my wife and get acquainted."

"But not Kat." I said, still miffed.

"Helen already knows Kathryn," he said, "In fact, that's the whole point of this meeting."

I muttered, "I don't get it. Somebody enlighten me."

"Okay," said Tony, "It's understandable that you only know Norma through Kathryn's eyes—what she thinks—what she says to you. But there's another side to Norma that I believe you should understand. And it's Helen that can 'enlighten' you, as you said. Take over, Helen."

She did. "Kathryn and Norma are much alike in some respects," she said, "and totally different in others. Neither has any tolerance for injustice, and yet they manage it beautifully, against each other.

"It makes sense if you give it some thought, and that is what we hope you will do. Give it some thought! Kathryn and her brother were never close, which doesn't help much, since it means they don't socialize much.

"And Kathryn has always felt that Norma not only took Richard away from the rest of the family, but that she also disapproves of Kathryn's lifestyle.

"Neither is true, but this is basically what Kathryn sees and feels."

She continued, "Richard lives in his own little world and wouldn't have done the 'family' thing anyway. Oh, each invites the other for dinner occasionally, but it remains pretty formal. Until you came to town Kathryn just took them out a couple of times a year. She's not much of a cook, as you've probably discovered.

"Norma, on the other hand, loves to entertain and really puts on the dog, as Tony would say—fancy table settings—fancy food—you know the kind. But she does it because she enjoys it, not for the sake of showing off.

"And it takes a lot more than an occasional dinner to really get to know someone, which is something they just haven't done. Richard, I don't believe, even notices the chilly atmosphere that surrounds the two women."

"Strange how a professional like that can hear and empathize with everybody else's problems, and not see the one at home," said Moira.

"Right." Helen resumed what I was now considering 'her little lecture'.

"I'm sure, from what Tony has repeated to me about his conversations with you—which I hope you will forgive him for—unlike a lot of couples, we really do talk to each other.

"Anyway, Kathryn thinks Norma is just a socialite who will do most anything to make news and get her picture in the paper, or on the television."

I said, "And isn't that correct? I seem to be seeing her face in the media all the time."

Helen said, "But have you ever taken special notice of just WHY she's in the news?"

"No, I guess I haven't." I admitted.

"Then start," she said, "Just about every time you see her, it's to promote some worthwhile cause. She helped raise funds for the new hospital wing, and for the children's free clinic. She was instrumental in getting new, safe playground equipment in two of our city parks, and just where do you think Tony got Duchess?"

I said, "I guess I never thought about it. I picked Mutt up at the shelter, but Duchess is purebred. At least she looks like it. I just thought you bought her somewhere."

"We did," Tony laughed, "We bought her at the Save the Greyhound shelter promoted by Norma Banks. That all began when she saved King Charles III from execution. He was only a day away from being put down for failing to win races. That riled her up and she began her campaign to get more of them adopted.

"Even the Gianellis," added Tony, "They have two. Nobody ever told the whole story, but that's what he was doing the day he was killed. Walking one of the dogs."

"There was no dog there," I protested.

"No, of course not. It ran off, and actually found its way home two days later. The blood on its coat was Gianellis. The lab confirmed it. Too bad it didn't get a chunk off the murderer."

I said, "What's too bad is that greyhounds are so unaggresive. He should have had a pit bull!"

"He used to," replied Helen. "It was TOO aggressive and he had to get rid of it."

"Now all of this," I waved my hand around the table, "Is to convince me to become the peacemaker?"

"On, no, my dear," Tony replied. "It's just to make you see things in a different light. Don't let Kathryn's insecurities influence you."

I felt like yelling at him, but this being a public place, merely said, although not very politely, "She doesn't have any!"

Moira decided it was time to enter the fray, "Oh, Ellie, don't be silly. Everyone has some. Even you."

"Me, yes, but it's my lack of education."

Tony intervened again "You've got all you need, girl. You have compassion, kindness, common sense and wisdom few people acquire with the aid of a diploma. All we are suggesting is that you now use it and see if it doesn't somehow bring Kathryn and Norma to some kind of understanding, just by osmosis, or something. Just let your own feelings rub off on the two of them, and time will take care of the rest."

I asked Helen, "And how did you come by all YOUR wisdom and information?"

"Easy," she said, "Norma was my college roommate. Neither of us aspired to sorority life, and lived our entire four years in one dorm room. We were, and still are, just a couple of ordinary gals and she's a great friend to this day."

Dinner arrived, along with much to think about in the days ahead.

The waiter had placed our tab on the table. I'd noticed before that this isn't one of those places where he takes it and brings back your change. It appeared to have a big turnover in servers, probably college kids trying to make a buck. You do add your tip to it, however, and pay at the cash register.

The gentlemen usually behind that computerized gadget was a distinguished looking middle aged fellow, very polite and friendly. His name I now learned when Tony tried to pay the bill, was Howard.

Howard tore up the bill, waved briefly toward a young woman I'd seen talking to him a few minutes earlier. She looked vaguely familiar, but I couldn't remember why.

Tony seemed to understand and mouthed a 'thank you' in her direction. She merely smiled and turned away.

Before I could follow the others out, Howard said, "Miss Lee? It's nice that you are getting acquainted in our town, first with Miss Banks and now with our favorite Judge. I hope we see you often."

He held out his hand. I couldn't possibly see what this gesture was about, but when I responded and pulled my hand away, I found a small folded note had been pressed into it. I quickly tucked it in my pocket before anyone else could see it. Obviously that was his intention, and although my curiosity was killing me, I'd wait to read it later.

The note read: "Please Help. Call this number at 6:00 p.m. today." and gave a telephone number. I couldn't tell if it was a landline or cellphone number, but I'd certainly call it at the designated hour!

The afternoon dragged on—

Moira noticed, and kept giving me funny glances. I finally decided I could used some input and showed her the note. "This was slipped into my hand at the restaurant."

"And you do intend to make the call?"

"Of course. How can anyone ignore a plea for help?"

She said, "You can't, of course, but there's no need to worry about it until after you find out what somebody's problem is."

"I'll continue to worry anyway," I said. Which I did.

Kat was late coming home. I fixed us a quick snack, just in case the phone call took us away through supper time, and left a plate for Kat in the refrigerator.

The hour finally arrived and I took out my cell phone, since it could be put on speaker and Moira could listen.

When a young-sounding female voice said a tentative "Hello?" I said, "This is Eleanor Lee. I was asked to call this number at 6:00. How can I help?"

"Oh, Miss Lee, I just couldn't think of anyone else to talk to. I'm Susan Gianelli. I really shouldn't bother you, but the day of Daddy's visitation when you told Eva you'd help, I somehow thought you meant it. I mean, people say things like that all the time, but it's only to be polite and what they really mean is they are sorry, but don't call. I really thought you meant it. Did you?"

"Of course dear. I'm to assume that you are the young lady I saw at the funeral home?"

"Yes. I almost spoke to you then, but chickened out. Eva would have heard. Then when I saw you at the restaurant this noon I asked Howard to slip you a note. I just don't know what to do! I'm scared!"

"What of?" I asked.

"Everything I guess. And everybody."

"I suppose that's natural, due to your father's murder. Is your mother frightened too?"

I heard a sort of gasp, then she said, "Oh, Eva's not my mother. And No, she's not one bit frightened. I guess that's part of why I am."

Moira was making gestures and trying to mouth words at me. I'm no good at lip reading but finally got it, "Where are you, dear? I think perhaps we'd better get together and discuss your difficulties."

"I'm in the restaurant parking lot. In my car. I don't know where to go."

I asked, "Do you feel safe inside the restaurant?"

"As long as Howard is there, yes."

"Then go back inside and wait. A friend and I will pick you up. I'll phone you again when we get there. Just come out and get in my car—it's a white Camry, and I'll stop in front of the door until you come out. Okay?"

"Okay."

We'd scarcely come to a stop before the frightened child made a dive into the back seat and hunkered down as if afraid of being seen.

"Where are we going?" she asked.

"Home," I replied.

"Oh, no," she gasped, "I can't go home."

"My home," I told her. "We can talk there."

"Are we being followed?"

It was Moira who replied, "No, child, we are NOT being followed."

An indignant voice said, "I'm not a child! And how do you know?"

"Because nobody followed us from the parking lot, and we haven't picked up a tail since leaving there."

"And you know all this because???"

"Because I do. Now, if you want to slouch down in that seat all the way, be my guest, but you look uncomfortable," said Moira.

The girl continued to keep out of sight, and said nothing as we drove home, where Moira said, "You have a bad habit of parking in the driveway, Eleanor. This time put it in the garage."

She turned to Susan "There's a direct entry from the garage into the kitchen. Nobody can see you."

Once inside, I pulled out a chair and directed her to "sit here Susan" and handed her one of Kat's diet sodas before starting a pot of coffee. I avoided calling her 'child' although that's what she seemed to be. Probably older than she looks, I thought, maybe about eighteen.

To me, a kitchen table is the perfect place for a conversation. It's easier to maintain eye contact, since nobody ever wants to deliberately get up and turn their back on you, as they are apt to do in the living room, where there always seems to be a window that must be looked out of when they want to avoid being 'read' by a good observer.

"Now," I said, "tell all, beginning with why you said Eva is not your mother."

"My mother died when I was seven. Daddy married Eva about a year later, said I needed a mother." For the first time, she laughed, but it didn't sound like it was from good humor. "I did, of course. I just didn't get one."

Moira chimed in, "And whose fault was that? How much did resentment come into play? I ask because this is so often the case, and men just don't seem to catch on."

"Okay," Susan replied, "I suppose I wasn't the best stepdaughter in the world. But I tried, I really did. It just wasn't the same, ever again. Mom used to read to me, and Daddy had done it after she died. Eva said I was old enough to read for myself, and he quit. I'd sometimes go crawl onto his lap in the evenings he was home, and of course she said I was too big for that too! It wasn't the reading, or the sitting on his lap, it was—well I guess I'd call it the companionship, the caring, that I needed, and it stopped.

"Mom took me shopping when she went. She asked what I'd like for dinner, and if it wasn't too outrageous, she fixed it. By outrageous I mean I couldn't have cake, ice cream, pie AND cookies and nothing else. We went to the park, and the zoo, and she came to visit school occasionally and talked to my teachers.

"She'd arranged for swimming lessons, and Eva canceled them. Daddy said she probably knew best, and never did override any of her decisions. I just felt abandoned, first Mom left me, and now Daddy was turning over everything to Eva. I had a hamster and he disappeared. She said he died."

"Well," I said, "I guess that explains that. So what's up now that has you scared?"

She hesitated, then said, "I guess it's partly Kenneth."

"Who's that?" asked Moira.

"Eva's youngest brother. She moved him into the house immediately after Daddy died."

I said, "She probably thought she needed somebody to help her."

"Maybe. But he creeps me out. Looks at me like I suspect a cat looks at a mouse. Not that I'd know. I never was allowed to have a cat either."

This seemed to be another cause for major annoyance. I'd probably have felt the same, but then, our house usually had two cats and a dog. And a lot of my friends.

"And now you are wanting to move out?" I asked.

This time she did laugh, "Oh, I already did that. You see, Daddy's funeral was in the morning, and in the afternoon Eva insisted on a formal reading of the Will. Everybody was there, her family, some of the restaurant personnel and household staff that she knew he'd left something to, me, and the lawyer, of course. She didn't know she'd left one out, but Daddy's attorney knew, and he brought along the man from the bank.

"The lawyer read the Will, and that's when things turned ugly. I thought Eva would explode, and the faces of her brothers boded no good either."

"How come?"

"She thought she knew what was in it. You see, several years ago I walked into Daddy's home office and found her sitting at his desk, reading something that even I, just a kid, would recognize as some kind of legal document. She made no attempt to hide it, so I asked, "What's that, Eva?"

"She said it was Daddy's Will, and since she needed to make one herself she was reviewing it in order to help her in planning her own. Then she said I was not to concern myself about it, since he'd made very good provision for me if anything happened to him.

"I said the desk drawer didn't seem to be a very safe place for it, and she told me the original was in the safe, this was only a photocopy that he'd kept at home.

"Later, when she was out, I dug it out and read it. He'd left everything to Eva, and after her, to me. There was a trust, for me, which I didn't really understand at the time, but it also said Eva would be my guardian, and trustee of the trust. I guess that's why I said he'd left everything to Eva. That's not literally true, but since she controlled the trust, it seemed so to me."

Moira said, "In other words, Eva would have control of absolutely everything."

"That's right. Including ME! What she didn't know was that he'd made a new Will about two years ago and only left her the house and half of the cash assets. The restaurant, other half of cash, plus my trust, would all go to me. And the banker who was present, together with Howard, would be trustees until I was twenty-one."

"Howard?" I exclaimed, "The man from the restaurant?"

"Yes. His full name is Lewis Howard, but everyone calls him Howard. He's been with Daddy since the first restaurant opened and become a trusted friend. He's also been like a second father to me.

"Anyway, Eva and the brothers reactions scared me so badly I packed a bag and got out of the house. I spent the first night in a motel, but didn't feel very safe there either, and besides, I didn't have sufficient cash on hand to keep paying for it. I'm sure Howard would have given it to me, but I just bought a pillow and sleeping bag and I've been sleeping on the office floor at the restaurant ever since."

I asked, "And you feel safe there?"

"I did. Until today. Now I can't stay there either," she replied.

"What happened today?"

"Kenneth walked in, told Howard he'd be closing up from now on and to just 'show him the ropes' and he could start tomorrow. Howard wouldn't have to do it any more, is what Kenneth said, he could just open in the morning and leave after the lunch hour. Kenneth would take over then and stay for the evening.

"I admit Howard can't keep on with his present hours. He's been coming in at 6:00 a.m. and not leaving until about 11:00 p.m. since Daddy died.

"But Howard simply told him not to bother. He'd continue to take care of it until the new owner found a replacement. Howard and Daddy had taken turns, all these years, arranging shifts to suit the convenience of both of them. They got along great and the system worked.

"Kenneth just turned a little red and repeated that he'd take over as of tomorrow afternoon, and that he'd be back tonight to help close up and take the day's receipts to the night deposit box. Anyway, that's when I realized that Howard and I didn't have the only keys. The police had turned Daddy's possessions over to Eva, and that included his keys.

"Wow! I see why you are upset."

"Howard simply told him not to bother, that the usual Security people would pick them up for deposit. Daddy had for many years not wanted any one person to have to assume the responsibility, and the risk, of transporting a lot of cash. Of course a lot comes in the form of credit card slips, but there is still quite a bit of cash.

"Oh, gosh, Miss Eleanor, how could I forget? Howard is closing up tonight, and I'm willing to bet that Kenneth, and possibly a few brothers, will walk in and try to take over. I've got to go back. Can you take me, right away?"

"Got a better solution, if I can locate him."

I got Chris on the phone and said, "Chris, I need a very big favor."

I explained the situation as succinctly as possible and he said, "Don't worry about it, Aunt Ellie. I'll be there to escort Mr. Howard safely home, and be sure the money goes, as usual, with the Security company."

"Uniform and squad car?" I asked.

"Yep, and probably a buddy or two. Perhaps nothing will go wrong, but we can't be certain of that, so you leave it to me."

We did.

Moira being more Susan's size, loaned her some pajamas, and we got the girl to bed, knowing we probably couldn't keep her here either. If she was in danger, this place was secure enough for us, but didn't have enough to protect her from any of Eva's determined relatives.

Telling myself to 'do a Scarlet' and think about it tomorrow, we all went to bed. I didn't, however, think about it tomorrow. What other safe arrangement could be made for Susan?

Needless to say I didn't sleep well, and didn't get up at my usual early hour. I was still in my pajamas and robe, starting the coffee, when Chris arrived. His face told it all. I debated getting Moira and Susan up, then decided against it. Let them sleep. I'd listen to his story.

He'd called a buddy who was on night duty, been picked up and the two of them walked into the restaurant just before closing time. Squad car at door, uniforms, badges and guns conspicuously present, and asked Howard if it was too late to get a snack.

Kenneth and one other man, closely resembling him, were there and informed them the place was closed for the night.

Howard said that for a couple of hungry officers, he'd rustle up a sandwich and some pie, but could they settle for a soda instead of coffee? The pots were already being cleaned. Chris said that would be great and they sat down at the table nearest the cash register. Kenneth seemed to want to hover over it, so neither turned their back on him, or it.

The clean-up crew left, and only Howard, Kenneth & Co., Chris and Buddy were there when the Security van drew up. The officers dawdled over their drinks while Howard made up the deposit, and they walked out with him while the security men accepted the bag and drove away.

He said Kenneth & Co. looked furious, but there was little they could do about it, since the two officers simply sat in their squad car apparently checking with the Police Dispatcher on the radio until everyone was gone except Howard, and they followed him home.

"Great work, Chris, but where does she go from here? She's too young to have to deal with this hassle."

"She's got to find help. Possibly Mr. Howard knows someone. But I haven't told you the whole story."

Chris had gone home, called three of his fellow officers from the early shift, explained the problem, and the four of them had turned up as soon as the restaurant opened. Sure enough, Kenneth & Co. were already there, hassling Howard.

"I just walked in, said 'my usual breakfast, Howard', and left the other three to order. One said that was fine with him too, one asked for pancakes and ham, the other said he'd rather have waffles, and was there any of that good black raspberry syrup? Just like we are there every morning before our shift.

"Howard didn't bat an eye. I had no idea what my 'usual' would turn out to be and frankly I didn't care. I'd eat it even if I hated it. I didn't. It turned out to be a great western omelet with toast, orange juice, coffee, and pancakes on the side!"

"Sounds like you might go back," I commented.

"Yep. He tried to make it on the house, but we, of course, can't accept. I told him he could just put it on your tab," he grinned.

"You certainly may, dear, indefinitely if it will help."

I reported to Susan and Moira when they finally got up, suggested they both stay in the house until I got back from my morning walk, after which I'd take Susan anywhere she wanted to go, and she said "to the restaurant" as she needed to talk to Howard.

Moira asked if she could use my computer, since I had internet access and she hadn't yet connected her laptop, and Mutt and I left for the park.

I was a little later than usual and hoped Tony hadn't left. He hadn't, but that's because he'd never been there.

Instead, I found Helen sitting on the bench, Duchess dozing at her feet. I wondered what was the reasoning behind this, but merely sat down beside her.

"Have you see the Daily Rag yet this morning, Eleanor?" she asked.

"No, sorry. Something in it I should know about?"

"Yes."

"Okay. Just a minute while I tie Mutt up. He's a little unruly this morning and I don't trust him." I carried a short extra leash in my bag, looped it around the leg of the bench, then hooked it to his long lead. He gave me a dirty doggy look and I apologized to him and promised to make it up with treats when we got home. He went as far as the leash permitted and harassed the ducks, as usual. Duchess ignored him.

"What's up?" I asked.

She handed me a newspaper, neatly folded back, "It's in the gossip column."

"I never read that anyway. I guess I just don't know enough of the local people to be interested in it."

She said, "Check out the part I marked."

It read:

*"Who is the pretty blond our favorite judge was seen lunching with yesterday? Anybody knows, call this reporter."*

There was a picture of the four of us at Gianellis but since it only showed the backs of Helen and Moira, the insinuation was that I was seeing Judge Essex and there might be a juicy tidbit to be gleaned.

"This is ridiculous. Helen, there's nothing going on...."

She interrupted, "I know that. You know that. Tony knows that. And after all the years you've been together, I presume Kathryn knows that. The problem is that about ninety-nine percent of the people of Charlotte don't know that."

"Oh, surely not that many read it," I said.

"The only ones besides you are those too young to read. Gabby's catty, but popular."

I asked, "And it's embarrassing to Tony?"

"I said I was going to set her straight, and Tony said just leave it alone and let it go away," Helen replied.

My imp surfaced and I proclaimed: "I've got a better idea. You know about making lemonade from lemons? Gianellis can do a great advertisement out of it, with Tony's permission of course. The paper could enlarge this picture and say 'Judge and wife (back to camera) with friends enjoy lunch at GIANELLIS (LARGE BOLD PRINT) followed by the address, hours open from six a.m. until ten p.m., Great Food. Blondie recommends the key lime pie. Come in and try it.' I'll run it past Susan and see if she wants to do it."

"Oh, Eleanor, that's hilarious. But who and what is Susan?"

Which meant I had to explain Susan, the Will, Eva and her brothers, Howard, Chris and his buddies interventions (two so far), Susan's current lack of safe housing, and the fact that apparently the girl's fears are not unfounded.

"She's at our house at the moment, but that can't keep on. We have absolutely no security system, but I suppose we could put one in, for what it's worth."

Helen said, "And she needs to find help for Howard, both relief on the job, and his safety, both on and off the job. If Susan owns the restaurants, and Howard is her trustee, both of them are at risk. If anything happened to Susan, Eva, as the grieving widow and mother, would automatically take over everything. And if something happens to Howard she could probably get the trusteeship back."

"My thoughts exactly. I wouldn't be so concerned if Kenneth & Co., as Chris calls them, hadn't been continually turning up. They seem rather persistent."

"And dangerous. I know the family reputation, although nothing has ever been proven against any of them. I just don't know why Gianelli ever married her in the first place."

My reply, "Well, you have to admit she's gorgeous. And he was no doubt lonely after losing his wife."

"And Susan is the only child. I know the feeling. I lost our only child and ended up with what my mother-in-law called 'parts missing'—all the important parts. Tony and I just decided there were kids out there needing a home and we'd adopt. Our son is currently about 600 miles away so we don't see him often. We do keep the phone and the e-mail busy."

"Tony mentioned a son. I didn't know he was adopted."

"We tend to forget that too. He's ours, it's as simple as that," she said.

She continued, "I'd like to meet your Susan. Let me take you home and perhaps we can figure out some solutions."

I untied Mutt. Duchess was awake now and industriously licking Mutt's silky ear.

"Make hay while you can, Duchess," I said, "he goes to the vet on Tuesday."

Helen said, "She's spayed, Eleanor."

"I know," I replied. "I was just teasing her. I firmly believe animals understand English."

"Except for those who understand French, Spanish, German...."

"Okay," I said, "at least we agree."

"My suggestion," said Helen, as we gathered around the kitchen table, "is Norma."

I'd fixed breakfast, made more coffee. Now, with fork almost to face, I sputtered and gasped, "Norma?"

"Until you finally figure it out for yourself, it seems I must keep telling you that Norma is not who you think she is—which means who Kathryn thinks she is."

I asked, "So what's she got to do with Susan's problems?"

"She's got the house."

"The house?"

"You've been there, Eleanor. It's practically a fortress. Norma would take Susan in, and she'd be safe there until the police catch her father's killer, or killers, and we think she's in no further danger herself."

"I've wondered about that house. Why does Richard need such an elaborate security system? And what makes you think they'd take Susan in?"

She replied, "The place was already that way when they bought it. It had been built by a very wealthy, and totally paranoid, old lady. The house was full of valuable art work and antiques. Her table was set, even when she ate alone, which she usually did, with sterling silver and Bavarian china. Her evening snack was brought to her room on a silver tray by the only servant she trusted to live full time in the house.

"All the other help were checked in at their appointed time, did what they came for, and checked out, either by her or the one she trusted."

I thought anybody who really tried could get over the fence, and said so.

She laughed, "They might. They might even survive it, but they'd wish they hadn't. Richard hasn't used it since they've lived there, but by pushing one switch in the gatehouse, the top of the fence is electrified. Norma would just love an excuse to turn it on."

"How and when did they get this fantastic place? And frankly, WHY would they want it?"

Helen said, "The old girl died and the place came on the market. She had a few relatives, but none she wanted to acknowledge with bequests. It seems they only paid attention to her when they wanted something, and she thought she'd given them enough.

"Everything she had was converted to cash and given to her favorite charities and a lot of research facilities. Richard figured the house was within a decent price range. As you know, the house itself isn't excessively large, not too costly to maintain, and Norma tells me the mortgage will be paid off in another two years.

"As to WHY they wanted it, the security did play a large part in their decision. Richard deals with a lot of people with mental disabilities, and occasionally some of them get contrary and he'd had some threats.

"Oddly enough none of the patients ever made actual trouble, but a relative of one did. The guy was conservator for a patient, had total control over both the patient and his assets, and feared losing that control if the patient was cured. Since he was improving rapidly, the relative decided Richard was to blame and actually 'lost it' and broke into their house one night.

"He was threatening Richard with a knife when Norma sneaked up behind and bonked him with the toaster. He hadn't either heard or seen her. She always did move quietly. Prefers to wander in her bare feet. Norma's son Danny used to joke that she did it to sneak up on him and catch him in mischief, but I know it pre-dates Danny by many years. Dorm life discouraged wandering the halls barefoot, but the minute she got back in our room her shoes were kicked off."

I exclaimed, "Helen, that's a tall tale and I don't believe it of Norma."

"Then you'd better start, because we are going to ask her to take Susan in, and we are doing it right now.

"Anyway, the place came on the market about that same time, and they decided to make an offer."

"If nobody can get in past the gate, or over the fence, how about dropping in by helicopter?" As aunt to a girl who owned one, I was very much aware of the capabilities of a good chopper pilot.

Helen said, "In THATcase I suspect Norma would just unleash the rockets or something."

We left the dogs in our back yard, picked up Susan and headed for the Banks' residence, or fortress, as Helen had called it.

Much to my amazement, Norma was instantly enthusiastic, fell immediately in love with the adorable Susan and said, "Get your stuff. You're moving into our guest room this very day!"

She was barefoot when she opened the door, and wearing blue jeans and t-shirt which proclaimed "Go Bears!"

I reckon (to use Shell's newly acquired Western word) I'll have to revise my opinion of Kathryn's sister-in-law after all.

After learning that Susan had taken almost nothing with her from home, she asked, "How much do we have to move? Do we need a U-Haul?"

"Just my clothes and a few personal items. We can probably get it all in the back of an SUV or station wagon," Susan replied.

"What will we want? Boxes? Bags? Or just spread a clean sheet in the back of my van and dump things on it?"

"That will work," said Susan, "I can clean and sort later. There's probably stuff I should donate to Good Will anyway. Should we get some off-duty police or something?"

Norma asked, "Are you that scared of Eva? Well, I'm not. If she won't let us in to retrieve your belongings, then it will be time to get reinforcements. Let's go, kid."

We went. But with four of us going, we decided to take both Norma's van and Helen's SUV in order to have more space. The kid might have more than we anticipated that she wanted to take with her.

Faced with four determined women, one of which had a very familiar face, it being so often in the news, Eva was more than cordial. A man I presumed to be Kenneth hovered in the background as we packed and hauled Susan's things to the two vehicles.

Eva said, "Susan, dear, you really don't have to do this. You are more than welcome to stay here. It's always been your home, and you can stay if you like, at least until you finish college."

"Thanks, Eva, but the house is yours now and I might as well get used to living on my own. I'm of age, and have funds enough, plus the income from the restaurants, to take care of my needs, including college expenses."

Norma added, "And of course, we are willing to help with anything Susan needs."

Anticipating questions from Eva, she quickly added, "Well, if that's everything you want to move, Susan, let's get going. I have a couple of things I still need to do today, not that I mind taking the time for you, dear, but could you please get a move on?"

Susan did—but not until a trip to the attic. She came down carrying what appeared to be a large picture frame, wrapped in brown paper. She said, "I know you don't want this, Eva, so I'm taking it."

"Fine, dear."

All this 'dear' business was becoming a little sickening, especially coming from those we knew didn't mean it.

Susan loaded her last item into Norma's van and we all returned to the fortress, where my first question was "Just what was it Eva wouldn't want?"

She unwrapped a portrait of a pretty woman who looked so much like herself that we knew it had to he her mother.

We immediately hung it over Susan's bed.

Richard and Deeanna were home, and Deeanna offered to help sort and hang Susan's clothes in the large closet.

Neither had been informed of Norma's plan to bring the girl home. Neither did of either of them question her decision. I suspected they never did. If 'mother' thought it was right, then it undoubtedly was.

It took the two girls about an hour, after which they came down the stairs dragging a large bag which was destined for the Salvation Army, or Good Will, or some such place. Norma suggested taking it first to the women's shelter, and anything that could be used there could be donated to the women.

Norma does seem to be full of good ideas.

We were just sitting around enjoying one of those companionable silences (all except for Deeanna and Susan, who were off in a corner chatting) and I was feeling guilty about not having been home to get dinner for Kat when Norma said, "Let's just fix everybody one last cup of coffee before we break up this unusual party."

Susan heard it, said, "Oh, No!" and jumped to her feet. "I completely forgot. I have to leave immediately!"

"Why, dear?" asked Helen.

"Because it's getting late and Howard will be closing the restaurant by himself. I just don't want him there alone."

That's when I discovered that Richard only seems to be in his own world. He's there all the time, just quietly lets everything go past him unless it's important.

He stood up and said, simply "Then what are we waiting for? We'll all go have that coffee at Gianellis."

Car keys in hand, he started for the door. Everyone followed. It also seemed that most of us reached for cell phones to call someone. I called Kat and she agreed to meet us there. Deeanna and Susan rode with Richard and Norma. Moira and I jumped in with Helen. Tony arrived ahead of us, so it was obvious who Helen had called. Kat followed shortly after us.

It was nearly closing time, but Howard greeted us, friendly but tired. "Susan said to leave the coffee on. You might also find some left-overs in the kitchen if you care to explore." So Susan had phoned him. I was guessing who Deeanna had called, and my guess was correct. We'd gotten our coffee, raided the kitchen, where I found lots of goodies and spread them out buffet style. We all helped ourselves, pulled a couple of tables together and sat down.

The door opened again and a familiar male voice said, "Party started without me?"

Deeanna moved over and he pulled a chair in beside her. "The party starts in the kitchen. Help yourself and come back."

He did, carrying a sandwich and large helping of cherry pie and saying, "Still having a problem, Howard?"

"How so?"

Chris replied, "Familiar car in the parking lot with two dudes sitting in it. I just can't believe they are customers whose vehicle won't start."

Howard said, "Oh, them. Uh Huh. What you've started referring to as Kenneth & Co. They arrived about half an hour ago."

Richard decided it was time to get back in the act. "Sit down, Mr. Howard. We are going to stay until we've figured out a solution. You are dog-tired, obviously. And Susan is frightened. Chris and his friends can't continue to open and close with you. You and Susan need additional security, and restaurant help."

"I can open in the morning," said Susan, "if there's enough security. I know how, you know. I've worked here after school and during summer breaks for years. Then you (pointing to Howard) can come mid-afternoon and finish up the day."

"No dice, honey," he replied, "You'll be going off to college and I can't let you do this. Your Dad's estate won't be settled for months. There will be too many complications and no doubt lots of challenges made to it."

"I'll delay college for a year, after everything settles down."

Kat spoke up, "There's another solution."

I said, "There certainly is." As usual, she knew exactly what I was thinking. I do believe she's been reading my mind from the day we first met in front of that shoe store, which, by the way, is still there. I go in often.

"Then let's hear it," said Tony.

"Me!" I said, "I'll open."

"That's ridiculous," was Howard's reaction.

"Absolutely not," was Tony's, "We can't let you do that."

"And why not?" I asked. "For several years I ran the country club back home, both cooking and service. I admit it was only part time, and much smaller, but the principle is the same. Moira, for as long as she's here, can bring me and pick me up, or I can drive myself. Susan, until college begins, can come show me the ropes and take care of the customers and cash register, and that gives her time to find, or choose from present employees, someone to take over. Howard does second shift with the safety of another security guard on the premises for at least the last hour, until the Brink's truck arrives. It's the perfect solution."

Some looked dubious. Not Kat, who knew me best. And not Susan who said, "Great. You're hired. We start tomorrow."

I'd gotten myself a job.

After a vain attempt to explain to Mutt that we would take our walk later, I picked up Susan and we headed toward the restaurant.

Moira had bowed out, stating that she'd walk Mutt briefly around the block and asking to use my computer again.

"Sure," I said, "use it any time. You don't have to ask. But what are you looking for?"

"Evidence." was all she said.

Why was I not surprised to see Chris and a friend sitting in his car in the parking lot? Has he adopted us, or was it the restaurant? I had noticed he was enjoying his meals there. In any event, it was reassuring to both of us and we invited them in for breakfast (on me, of course). But why was I also not surprised to see that Howard had already opened the place? I know he's extremely protective of Susan, but wondered also if he didn't really think we could handle the job. We'd just have to prove it, but it was nice to have him on this first day.

The rest of the morning staff would be arriving soon, but I fixed the omelet I already knew Chris liked so well, and another for his friend.

While they were eating I checked the menu for the day and inspected the refrigerator and freezer to make certain everything that had been ordered yesterday had been delivered. The kitchen was immaculate, but of course it would be, with Howard in charge.

The phone rang. Kat wanted to be certain that we'd arrived safely.

"Why wouldn't we?" I asked. "I do know how to drive, you know."

I figured she'd call continually if I didn't do something to discourage her. She worries too much about me.

As soon as I hung up it rang again. This time it was Moira asking the same thing.

This has got to stop!

Early customers began to arrive. Susan took charge of the dining room. I took over the kitchen. Howard hovered!

Except for the telephone we were doing fine, so I put him in charge of answering it, and after everyone we knew had called, we sent him home with orders to rest until time for his afternoon shift.

Mutt was missing Duchess. I was missing my morning visits with the Judge. Moira was still walking Mutt around the block and spending the rest of the time, it seemed to me, on my computer.

I tried to explain to Mutt that this was only temporary and things would get back to normal after Susan found a permanent morning manager, but he didn't believe me, and spent much of the evening sulking or sitting at Moira's feet. I told him his new friend wasn't permanent either, that she had a real job back in Wyoming and would eventually have to return to it. I think he understood, because he sulked even more. Kat brought him his favorite doggie treats and now everyone was in favor with him except me!

I asked Moira what she was doing all day on the internet and she said "Snooping." and said no more. I did notice, however, that Abe's e-mail address and web site had been added to my address list.

Everything else was going very well. There had been no further sign of Kenneth & Co. either IN the restaurant or OUT in the parking lot. Nor had we seen anyone who appeared to be tailing us, either coming or going. I continued to pick Susan up. She'd taken her car to the Banks' residence, but it was convenient, since I go right by their house anyway, and because we were trying to obey the Scout rule of buddy system.

Howard stayed away until time for his afternoon shift. Reluctantly.

Did I say everything was going well? It was, at least at work. BUT—

Wednesday evening I turned on the news and whose face should appear on the screen but Susan's! Some snoopy reporter with a camera crew had caught her coming out of her attorney's office with Deeanna.

She'd left work a little early to meet with him, and Deeanna, who had no patients that afternoon, had offered to drive and accompany her.

She was being bombarded with questions, some of them logical, although I knew they could have easily gotten their answers elsewhere, and some were downright impertinent and none of their business.

"Has your father's killer been found yet?" Obviously they knew he, she, or they, had not.

"How are you coping with your loss?" How would anybody who'd lost a father in such a tragic manner cope? None of their business.

"Are you going to operate the business yourself?" Of course she was. Why else was she here so early every morning.

"When will the estate be settled?" When the lawyers get done with it, obviously.

"Can the controversy over the estate be resolved?"

"What controversy?" was her answer. I was proud of her. Maybe I can be her aunt too.

"The division of property between you and your stepmother, of course."

"We aren't disputing the terms of my father's Will, so I guess the answer is still, what controversy?" she replied.

"But haven't you been kicked out of the house?"

"If you know so much about our affairs, you must know that I am of age. Daddy left both of us adequately protected. Eva loves the house. I don't. I still have fond memories, however, of the previous house, and if it ever came on the market I'd make an offer.

"And I love the business. Eva doesn't. Daddy knew all this. As to being kicked out, Eva has repeatedly invited me to stay, but since I'll be leaving for college this Fall anyway, decided I'd better get used to being on my own in the meantime. I left by MY choice, nobody else's."

"Who will operate the business when you leave?"

"I'm not sure yet. We are looking for a good restaurant manager."

"Who's now doing the chef's job? Surely you can't manage that at your age."

"You want to bet? If you can spare this much time bothering me, you might spare enough to come into my kitchen tomorrow morning and see for yourself who's doing it. I've been Daddy's girl all my life, so I've spent all my spare time since I was a kid in that restaurant, starting by washing dishes, cleaning tables, cooking, checking and ordering supplies, waiting tables, standing behind the cash register and making out the deposits. Don't sell me short."

"Who are you living with?"

"Friends. Now if you will excuse me, one of them is waiting for me."

She walked away.

YES! I'm definitely going to apply for job as auntie Ellie.

What's that they (whoever they are) say about the quiet before the storm? I should have known things were going too smoothly.

Well, at least they did until the following Monday. I dropped Susan off, returned home, walked in the door straight into the presence of a strange guy. A VERY strange guy indeed. He looked like a bandit in an old Western movie, wearing jeans, a pair of dirty, beat-up boots and with a red bandanna tied over his face for a mask. Mutt was nowhere to be seen, and oddly enough I found this comforting. If he was outside he wasn't in danger, and probably if he had been in he'd have been tail-wagging in friendly fashion anyway.

Moira was nowhere to be seen either, and this was NOT so comforting. Or was it? I couldn't be sure.

I barely recognize a rifle from a machine gun, but I felt like I was now looking down the barrel of a canon … at least it looked a lot like the Civil War one in the city park back home. Shell being a regular tomboy when she was small, used to love to climb on it. Of course I know this was just a small handgun—but they all look alike to me. And all of them are scarey.

"What do you want?" I gasped.

"Where is she?" was his answer.

"Who?"

"Oh.… nobody.… nothing. I mean, where do you keep your jewelry.… and cash?"

I was pretty sure this wasn't what his original question meant, but didn't intend to argue.

I started backing toward the living room, thinking there might at least be something I could use to protect myself. This hallway was pretty bare except for the little bench and a mirror on the wall. Neither looked promising.

He followed me, then stopped in his tracks as a calm but determined voice behind him demanded, "Drop your weapon."

He didn't—just kept moving toward me.

Moira repeated, "Drop your weapon. Do it NOW!"

Suddenly he became a believer, and I realized it was because Moira had moved into a position that allowed him to see her in the large hall mirror.

Her gun was pointed straight at him, and her hand was steady, her eyes cold. But he still held his weapon, until she said, "If I see your trigger finger move the tiniest bit, you're dead, mister."

He slowly lowered his gun, then dropped it.

"Now kick it away," she said.

He did.

"What's the matter, Moira, couldn't you find the toaster?" I asked.

"Huh?"

"Norma would have beaned him with the toaster."

"Oh. Her. Well, as you know, I'm not much good in the kitchen. But I'm real good on the target range, and believe it or not, Eleanor, I have shot two people. One of them is dead."

I noticed the effect of this statement upon our hapless captive. He started squirming and looking around as if for someone to rescue him. No such luck.

I started to reach for the weapon he'd dropped and Moira said, "NO! Don't touch it."

"Why not?"

"For starters, forensics don't really need any of your fingerprints. Just kick it farther away from him and back away."

"Can't I at least yank that silly bandana off him and see who we've got here?"

"Leave him be, Eleanor. Don't get near him until I tell you to."

I did as she said, kicking the little gun down the hallway in the general direction of the kitchen. Then I wished I hadn't. Suppose Mutt came in and added some of HIS DNA on it? Or worse, decided we were playing retriever and he picked it up?

Before that could happen, our prisoner suddenly said, "Would you two broads just shut up and decide what you are going to do with me? Call the cops? Listen to my hard luck story and let me go?" Not likely. "Go ahead, call the cops. I'd rather deal with them than with you two crazy women."

I told him, "First, I'd like to know what you really came for. Second, if you want my advice, don't use that term when you appear in Court, especially if you get a female Judge. You don't need a contempt charge added to your other follies, do you?"

Moira said, "He's right about one thing, Eleanor (she only calls me that when she means business, so I'd better listen), just stop talking and call the Police." (and she never uses the word 'cops', finding it offensive, I guess, although other police I've known don't seem to mind. Shell uses it all the time, and she's a former cop).

"How can I stop talking if I'm to call the Police. Why don't you do it?"

"Because my hands are otherwise occupied."

She was right.

I called.

They came.

He went when they did.

But before they arrived, Mutt finally decided to honor us with his presence. Thankfully, he totally ignored the new floor decoration our visitor had brought with him, but came dragging his leash.

It was pretty obvious what he wanted.

We used the leash to tie our perp to a chair.

Okay, so I've seen one too many cop shows.

Mutt sulked some more.

What a crazy day!

Helen practically followed me home the next day, having been informed of our latest adventures.

"Are you all right? Nobody was hurt?"

"We're fine," I replied, "Come on out on the porch and I'll get everybody some iced tea. It's too warm this afternoon for coffee."

"I've got Duchess in the car. Can I bring her in?"

"Sure. Mutt would no doubt appreciate that. He's been doing a lot of sulking since I started work. He misses Duchess, and our walks, and probably the ducks."

We turned the two dogs out in the back yard, which was enclosed by a high fence. Due to safety reasons, and the pool, we'd checked to be sure it passed inspection. It had also turned out to be a big advantage when I got Mutt, and I figured neither dog could jump over it.

I also know that any kid who really wanted to climb over and use the pool would figure out a way to do it. If convicts can scale high walls and slip through wire to escape, any five year old could get over this fence. Kat just increased our liability insurance and we went on enjoying it.

I brought out our tea, and a plate of oat bran muffins (Kat was watching my diet lately) and we settled in to watch Mutt and Duchess chase each other around the yard.

It being rather warm, Mutt eventually decided to cool off and jumped in. Pity the poor pool boy! There's lots of shaggy dog hair in our filtering system. On second thought, why pity him? If nobody needed their pools cleaned he'd have to find another job. He's a nice boy, trying to work his way through college.

Duchess circled the pool several times before deciding it wasn't worth it, and sat down at the shallow end to watch her frisky buddy.

He got out, eventually, and started shaking water all over her. She headed toward the safety of the porch and he followed.

I ran and latched the doggy door before they could get in. Rather than get Helen and I splashed, Mutt could just sprinkle the grass instead. Come to think of it, he did that frequently anyway, although not always with pool water.

Moira came out to join us. I pointed to the extra glass of iced tea, then to the papers she was holding in her hand, "What have you been doing?"

"Oh, these," she waved them at me, then brought them over and dropped them in my lap. "Susan said she didn't have any relatives left. I told Patrick that (Patrick being known to everybody else as Abe—but she said she'd named him Patrick and as his mother, would continue to call him that) and he said that was nonsense. Everyone has relatives somewhere, even if you had to go all the way back to Adam to find them. I just got these. He says it's only a partial list, just the closest ones, aunts, first cousins, etc.

"He also says Susan needs to make her Will, sooner rather than later, to protect herself, and this list might come in handy."

Helen says, "I've been hoping she'd do that too, and that her lawyer is doing it. If I was representing her, it would have been done immediately."

"You?" I asked, "you mean to tell me you're a lawyer?"

"Of course. What did you think I was?"

"Golly, Helen, so much has been happening, I reckon I didn't bother to think about it at all, beyond housewife. Did you and Tony go to school together?"

"No," she replied, "I met Tony when I joined his law firm. I knew from the first minute that I was going to chase him until he caught me, and flirted outrageously. It's a wonder I wasn't fired."

Moira said, "Looks like he appreciated it, since as you say, he caught you."

"So we got married, I became pregnant, quit work, lost the baby and learned I couldn't have any, became terribly depressed but didn't want to go back to the office. Then we got Greg and the lights came on in my world again. I stayed home until he started school, but did my continuing education, kept my license and since we don't need the money, I do a little pro bono work in my spare time.

"Now that Tony is on the bench.... I often wonder about that bench thing. Where did the expression come from? The chairs the Judges have look pretty comfortable to me.... I'm back, using his old office but still doing pro bono for people who can't afford representation. The firm kindly allows me use of any of the secretaries or legal assistants who might be available. It's good P.R. for the firm, and relieves the other attorneys from doing work for free. Somebody has to pay the overhead!

"Anyway, we will have to give this list to Susan, and ask if she's done anything about her Will."

Mutt returned to sulking after she and Duchess left, but at least he was getting fairly dry. A little toweling and TLC restored his usual good humor. A few of his favorite treats also helped.

Although everyone thought my idea for the advertising for Gianelli's restaurant was pretty cute, of course we all recognized that with Tony's position in the community, he'd have to veto the idea.

He did, however, come up with an idea of his own, which was to instruct Howard to let us know next time Gabby Gabrielle made a reservation, and we'd all go and have a big party in her presence.

That's how we all.... and by 'all' I mean Tony and Helen, Richard and Norma, Kat, Moira and I, plus Deeanna, Chris, his parents, three of Chris's police buddies, (the ones he'd brought to breakfast allegedly at my expense, although I've yet to receive a bill for it), plus Susan and Howard, made a total of sixteen of us gathered around several tables which had been pulled together.

We arrived before the Gabby one and were laughing, talking, and already digging into our food before she made her grand entrance.

Instead of everyone ordering from the menu, and thereby holding up time, we'd asked Susan, with Howard's help, to just choose what would be served to us. After all, they pretty well knew our likes and dislikes by now. The only thing we would pick for ourselves would be the dessert, and for that a waiter brings around a huge tray loaded with special goodies and the customer takes what he wants. If you REALLY wanted that cheesecake and the person ahead of you got the last piece, all you needed to do was ask and another would be brought. Now I call that service!

But let us return to Gabrielle. Being Queen of the World, she swooshed (that's the only expression I can think of for it) in, waved to everyone as if they were all special friends, and was escorted to her table. Incidentally, did I fail to mention that Howard had given her the table next to ours? She could therefore snoop, listen, make guesses as to who's who and otherwise make notes for tomorrow's column. It was extremely advantageous to all of us.

She glanced over, as though she hadn't already cased the room, pretended to see Norma for the first time, and 'swooshed' some more, over to Norma, who of course had probably the most recognizable face in the room, being seen so often on television or in the newspapers.

"Norma!" she gushed, "How nice to see you. I hear your save the greyhound project is going well."

"Just fine," said Norma, "We adopted out three more this month already. I was about to take the last one myself when a lovely young couple came in and took her."

"Would King Charles like company? I heard you had a problem with him recently."

"It's resolved, thank you."

She returned to her table, apparently waiting for a friend, but simply ordered a drink while waiting. And eavesdropping, of course. I hoped she misunderstood something which would cause her to put her foot in her mouth while writing it up.

I'm being catty. Most of the world loves gossip. I just don't appreciate being the source of it.

We were still there when she left, and we had a wonderful evening.

*Dear Shell,*

*Just thought I'd report in. I tried to phone, got your answering machine twice and gave up. What have you been doing?*

*Since driving Susan to work I've noticed that she's totally concentrated on the day ahead, menu planning, what supplies we need to order, that sort of thing.*

*She definitely doesn't want to discuss personal things early in the day, so I've learned to save those for the drive home.*

*I did give her the 'Susan's relatives' list that Abe sent through Moira, and asked if she'd done anything about making out her Will.*

*She said she'd discussed it with her attorney, but couldn't decide on beneficiaries. She didn't realize she had any close living relatives. She'd like to leave everything to Howard but he had told her not to.*

*Then she started making a list of possible charities or educational institutions, but hadn't come to any decisions.*

*Now, with a list of people she hadn't known existed, she was even more confused. It seems Abe had talked to a couple of aunts ad uncles, who were happy to have news of Susan. They had become estranged from her father after he married Eva.*

*She'd made it nearly impossible to maintain any family connections, either of his or of Susan's mother, and he'd given up trying.*

*They, on the other hand, didn't like her, and didn't trust her, so everything fell apart. Susan was pretty young at the time, hadn't seen any of her relatives for several years prior to her mother's death, and simply didn't remember any of them.*

*She asked if I had any advice. I told her to discuss it with Norma and Richard, and even Tony or Helen and she promised to do so.*

*Then I suggested she get in touch with some of the aunts, uncles and cousins and get acquainted.... see what she'd like to do about restoring the family relationship, but in the meantime if it were me, I'd go ahead and make the will, with charities as beneficiaries.*

*Later if she wants to change it and include relatives, she could. I reminded her that a LAST WILL AND TESTAMENT doesn't say 'final', and only the latest one counts, but she should do it sooner rather than later.*

*She promised. I hope she follows through.*

*Thanks for the pictures of Leeanna holding Lucky. She's growing so fast. The one where she's clutching Lucky is especially cute!*

*Love, Aunt Ellie*

Norma phoned me at work Tuesday morning asking me to come in for a few minutes when I brought Susan home, instead of dropping her off inside the gate.

After making a brief stop at a florists shop to order an arrangement sent to an old friend back home for her birthday, we arrived at Norma's door.

She met us with a big smile and "Guess what? I have good news!"

"We could use some," I replied, "We still don't have a good lead on a new assistant manager for the restaurant. Susan has had a couple of applications, but none Howard thinks are capable of doing the job.

"So what's your great news?"

She waved a paper at me and said, "Remember King Charlie's 'arrest' for allegedly biting another dog?"

"Of course I do. It, I believe, was the beginning of our friendship."

"It was. That's why I have to share this with you. I got a judgment against the nut who accused him."

"What?" I asked, "And how?"

"I was so annoyed, irritated—just plain angry Richard said, that he suggested getting it off my chest by filing a small claims lawsuit against her.

"So I found out who charged him, filed the suit, and went to Court this morning. The bill wasn't very big, just to the Veterinary Clinic for the bite casts and a couple of days of boarding for him.

"I wasn't mad about the money situation, but I was furious that anybody would make the charges, when I knew they weren't true, and she had to know it also. And I wanted to confront her to show her people wouldn't stand for that kind of thing.

"I also hoped to find out why she did it. It was just an attempt at extortion, as far as I'm concerned. She'd seen Richard walking Charlie, knew where we lived, forgot about our security system and that poor Charlie couldn't possibly have gotten out, and thought we had more money than the owner of the pooch that really bit her dog.

"Now she has to pay not only my Vet bills but her own."

"Payback time," I said.

"Yep, and I'm deliriously happy. Silly isn't it, but revenge really is sweet. Shouldn't be, of course, but I just don't seem to care."

I didn't seem to care either. She got her just desserts. Possibly very sour lemon pie—or chocolate cake someone put salt in by mistake instead of sugar—of even better, chocolate chip cookies made with ExLax instead of chips.

I stayed for a latte.

I got home to find an e-mail from Shell:

*Dear Aunt Ellie,*

*Glad you liked the photos.*

*We've been rather busy or I'd write more often. The twins, Joey and Josie, spent two weeks with us. Julie flew out to California and got them. Their grandmother came with them, and she's a delightful lady. We all had a wonderful time, and Leeanna got more attention than was good for her.*

*Then Brian came from Montana and brought his handicapped friend. He did some terrific sketches while he was here, of the ranch, the horses, and the people, mostly Leeanna. I'm getting them framed. It seems she's the biggest attraction around. Linda and Danny took all the kids riding. I wasn't surprised that Brian caught on so quickly, but Ernie was amazing, from the very first day. He loved the horses and they knew it. I actually think they miss him, and I know Mitch does.*

*The pool is almost done. We look forward to jumping in, especially when winter arrives again. Having it heated, covered, and the spa operating will be great. The underground tunnel from our basement out to it was finished and lighted last Thursday. The architect suggested making it wider than a regular tunnel, putting up some cabinets for storage of blankets, water, battery operated radio and lamps, plus extra batteries, and it would be a perfect storm shelter, since there's heat if the power doesn't go off, and ventilation if needed. We may never need it, but it does give a feeling of safety and is well worth the small additional cost. We plan to get a few more folding lawn chairs and store them there for use outdoors, or extras if we need them around the pool for visitors.*

*We will probably start pumping tons of water by the end of this week.*

*After leading such a frugal life, how did I ever get this lucky?*

*You haven't mentioned the murder problem lately. Has Susan signed her Will? I ask because, although I know Moira is enjoying her working vacation, Abe is making noises like he has a case he could use her on. He won't ask you to send her back, however, until you all think everyone is safe.*

*Love you all—————Shell*

The first instant she'd laid eyes on me, she knew.

And I knew she knew I knew.

To make it worse, she knew I knew she knew! Okay, enough already!

She seemed bewildered, stunned even, and didn't know what to say or do.

I, on the other hand, had rehearsed this scenario thousands of times in my mind. All I had to do now was choose one and use it.

So I smiled, held out my hand, said how happy I was to meet her and went on to discuss other of the inanities we women use when we first meet someone.

"Absolutely love your hairdo. Where do you get it done?" I asked. "Do they have someone who can cut curly hair? I have a terrible time finding a place that gets it right."

And she told me where she went, the name of her hairdresser, that she didn't know about cutting curly hair, and the usual "I think you're SO lucky to HAVE curly hair; you never have to sit through permanents, with chemicals running down your face. And the horrible smell!"

So much for small talk. I had no idea whether or not 'he' knew. I also had no idea how to find out without making the problem ten times larger than life!

Fortunately, there were other people present and the talk became general. I wondered if anyone there had sensed our temporary discomfort. I also probably should remove that word 'temporary' as I fear it will be ongoing until we find a way to resolve it.

And that will have to be done privately, not in front of a bunch of people whose business it is not.

I need somebody to re-write this redundant, confusing, ungrammatical chapter, but would have to do a lot of explaining before they could attempt it.

And I don't know how to tell it. Even IF I wanted to.

What a mess!

And likely to become worse before it gets better.

Norma had invited us over for dinner. Kathryn was either going to be late, or not able to come at all, having to show a house that evening. It was for a special client and she preferred not to have one of the other people from the office cover it, so I went on alone.

Moira had excused herself, saying she was waiting for an important call from her son.

I arrived a little early, and Norma led me into the living room, where Richard sat, as usual behind the evening newspaper.

She said, "The girls are fixing dinner tonight. Deeanna wants to learn to cook, and she's certainly not going to learn it from me, so she and Susan have been doing dinner lately. It's giving the housekeeper some much needed vacation time."

"The girls get along pretty well don't they, in spite of slight age difference?"

"Yes, they do. And I think having a 'big sister' is really good for Susan. She's really pretty much alone and has been for most of her life."

"Until she contacts those relatives," I added.

Richard spoke up, "She's signed her Will, finally, saying she'd done as you suggested, leaving a number of charities as beneficiaries until she meets the aunts, uncles, cousins, whatever she finds out there."

"That takes care of Eva plus Kenneth & Co. I guess. They now have no advantage in harming her. Tell her if you will, for me, that I realize she may not have funds until the estate gets completed, but if she wants to have a family reunion, that is, invite a bunch of them to come to town I'll foot the bill for their hotels and meals while they are here."

Richard said, "Oh, no, Eleanor. We'd take care of that. There's no need for Kathryn to pay it."

"Kathryn?" I asked, "What's she got to do with it? It's my idea and I can handle the arrangements. Maybe she'd like to have it before she leaves for college. Or possibly a big party at Thanksgiving."

Norma said, "But it would be expensive. You couldn't possibly…." She broke off suddenly, seemingly embarrassed and for once at a loss for words.

I finally caught on. "Oh, no! You didn't think.... you did, didn't you? Think Kathryn supports me?"

"We really don't mind that, Ellie dear," said Norma. "You mustn't think we resent it. Anything that makes the two of you happy is okay with us."

Suddenly I was Ellie dear instead of Eleanor. I should have been flattered. "But you DO think she foots my bills. Actually we split most things 50/50, including the house purchase. Did you think I was broke?"

"You've never worked much, couldn't have very much income."

"No, but between what Anna and Kevin both sent to Pops, and he kept it all, except for what we spent for Shell's education, it really piled up, with interest and all, and I was amazed to end up with a considerable fortune. It wasn't until Pops died that I learned that even Paul Rayburn knew about Shell and had created a trust for her. Shell refused to accept any of it when Pops died. I added what Pops had to the trust for her until she inherited the Rayburn estate, after which she insisted I use it. She said I'd earned it, all those years taking care of her, Mother before she died, and then Pops.

"Actually, you don't have to worry about me. I'm quite 'loaded' as Susan would say."

This strange little incident explained a lot about their previous relationship with Kathryn, which of course also meant hers with me.

They apologized if, as they said, they'd offended me. Actually I'd found it a trifle humorous, but didn't say so. "Frankly, I find it reassuring to know you accept me for myself alone," I told them.

The girls prepared a delicious dinner.

Kathryn got there just in time for dessert. It turned out to be Baked Alaska. Deeanna is really getting some lessons in cooking!

Strange things kept happening.

I was just leaving the restaurant, Susan having decided to stay for another couple of hours to meet with their bookkeeper, when a voice behind me asked: "Miss Lee, have you got a minute?"

I recognized the voice and wanted to say "No, I haven't," but honesty prompted the "Yes, what can I do for you?" I wasn't in any hurry and couldn't seem to bring out the lie.

Gabrielle asked, "Then can I buy you a coffee?"

"Sure," I replied, "This is the slow customer time but busy in the kitchen getting ready for dinner hour, so I'm sure I can rustle up a pot of coffee and a couple of cups, along with a few moments of my time."

I already knew she drank hers black so there wasn't anything else to get. While I was getting the coffee she chose a table and sat down.

"What's on your mind?" I asked.

Gabrielle said, "Well, as you know, I work for the newspaper." She laughed, "I guess that's been made rather obvious. Well, I just wanted, for starters, to tell you I'm not what I seem. I really like people, and try hard not to hurt anyone, although my publisher, editor, and the general public seem to have a different opinion."

I said, "I guess I wouldn't know. I've only read a couple of your columns. One incident annoyed me rather, but I must admit it wasn't slanderous."

"Thanks. Well, the reason I wanted to talk to you is this: I know you are only working here on a temporary basis, just to help Susan Gianelli until she finds a permanent employee, and I wondered if you had any ideas about your own future?"

"Just to go back to walking my dog at 6:00 a.m. instead of rushing down here," I said.

"Won't you get bored? I would, without something interesting to do."

"My life was not boring before work, and I don't expect it to get so after I quit," was my response.

"But would you LIKE to have a job? Maybe just a few hours a day?"

"Maybe," I said, "if it was something that I enjoyed."

"You like people," Gabrielle said, "And our food editor is leaving in a couple of months, moving, of all places, to Idaho."

I laughed, "Then perhaps she can do potato recipes."

"Probably," she laughed too. "But I had an idea and presented it to my boss. It's sort of like when Gabby Gabrielle first started—the first person doing the column really was named Gabrielle (mine, in case you don't know, is really Mary Ann Stokes). Anyway this young girl came to work for the paper and came up with the idea of picking people out at random and interviewing them. The person could pick any topic they wanted, as long as it wasn't something that was already being overdone by the media of the entire world, or she'd choose some small item from yesterday's paper and they would discuss it.

"She did several on her own time, showed them to the boss, who liked them and decided to try it out for a month. It caught on and ran for several years, and included her picture. People actually started approaching her for interviews.

"It began as 'Gabbing with Gabrielle' and only turned into a gossip column after she left. Two more people ahead of me had it, the last one being a man who was fired after a couple of lawsuits were filed against the paper. I'd like to turn it back to the original format, but the boss won't let me."

I asked, "Then why don't you try sneaking in just one a week and see how it goes?"

"Good idea," she said, "I might just do that."

"But I don't think that's what you waylaid me to discuss, is it?"

"No. It's the food column thing. I thought it would be something you might like to try."

"I'm not a nutritionist—I just like to cook," I said.

"That wasn't my idea. But I recently visited a nursing home with one of my friends. We found her mother and three other ladies at a table discussing their lunch. They weren't TOO critical, only started talking about things they'd liked, and fixed for their families years ago. One was from Iowa and started talking about 'cooking for threshers', which I gathered was when help came in for harvest season and the housewives got out the really big pots and pans.

"That's when it occurred to me that a really neat column could be written by interviewing older ladies, getting their histories, stories and recipes. You could get German, French, Italian, good old southern, the whole gamut and I think it would be a hit. The boss said he'd give it a try if I could find someone to do it."

"Actually," I said, "I was thinking of doing a cookbook. Something like 'Aunt Ellie's Gourmet made Easy'." I've got to get rid of that word 'actually', it's getting redundant.

She said, "You could do both, and the interviews might lead to a second book. Will you give it a try? You could even write them up at home and either e-mail or fax them in to the office."

"I'll think about it."

It sounded like fun.

At the door she paused again, "And, Miss Lee, the article which annoyed you really started "New Gal in Town?" and went on to pretty blonde lunching with our favorite Judge and his wife. I get edited too. By removing just three words it was turned from an innocent query into an insinuation. And as for my sailing in and out of places as though I owned the world and everything in it isn't me either. It's part of the Act.

"At least they didn't completely edit the picture. It was obvious there were other people at the table. But it is too bad they cut off the face of the handsome young waiter. He's really a cute kid."

I replied, "That's Johnny. Yes, and he's as nice as he looks. Including him would have been really good advertising. Probably would have brought in half the young girls in town and increased the volume of business tremendously."

"Then you have another good idea. Include pictures of your student employees, complete with name and school, their educational goals, etc."

I said, "Thanks. I'll make that suggestion to Susan and Howard."

And Gabby Gabrielle was really a nice girl. How often we misjudge!

Chris caught up with us at the park entrance. "Hey, Aunt Ellie, hold up a minute."

Mutt and I held up.

"What's up, Chris?"

"It's about the guy who got into your house. My Captain said I should tell you about him. It seems he was pretty high on crack...."

I interrupted, "I don't know much about drugs, but he certainly wasn't behaving in any fashion I'd call normal."

"Still isn't," he replied, "Anyway, it seems he was looking to fund his habit."

"Yep. He asked for money. We never have much cash in the house, but I suppose there are a lot of things he could have taken and sold."

"Probably. However, that wasn't what he really had in mind. It seems he'd heard a rumor on the street that anybody who brought Susan Gianelli in would be paid a cash sum of Ten Thousand Dollars. He apparently intended to accept the offer."

I exclaimed, "Wow! Is there really such an offer?"

"Nobody knows for sure, but the rumor is definitely floating around on the streets. Nobody is trying to collect, except this jerk, because it isn't known where to deliver her and collect."

"Well, I certainly hope nobody finds out."

"Me, too," Chris said, "And now that he's sobered up a bit, he admits he wouldn't have tried anything either if he'd been thinking properly. But he's still pretty spaced out, a total idiot and badly addicted."

I asked, "Where is he now? Still in Jail? In a treatment facility?"

"Still in jail and making everybody wish he wasn't. Going cold turkey in a cell isn't easy and he's driving everyone, including himself, absolutely crazy."

I said, "It almost makes me feel sorry for him."

"Don't feel TOO sorry, aunt Ellie. He could do a lot of damage."

"If he's too broke to feed his habit, how did he get the gun?"

"Stole it from a local sporting goods store, and it wasn't even loaded. He didn't manage to get away with the ammunition for it."

"If I'd have known that I'd have tackled him myself. Of course that would have completely spoiled Moira's fun."

He said, "Yeah. She sure enjoyed that. Well, anyway, somebody has to decide soon what they intend to do with him—get him off the jailer's backs, not to mention the effect he's having on the other inmates. The biggest worry now is still the rumor. It's still out there and Susan has to be extremely careful. Warn her, will you? Also Richard and Norma. I've talked to Howard but he can't do much when he's out of the restaurant."

I said, "Well, Chris dear, I have an idea. But it's conditional upon letting the story leak to the media. Can you get me that permission?"

"I'll let you know. But who are you intending to conspire with?"

"I'm not telling. Not until we get permission, and plans properly laid."

"Okay. But be careful, will you?"

"That's not exactly my middle name, but I'm working on it. Moira is still here and will help, and I think I've gained an ally at the newspaper. And that might lead to another ally at the TV station."

Chris left and Mutt and I resumed our walk.

We were disappointed that Tony and Duchess weren't at the far side of the duck pond, and Mutt seemed wary and anxious.

I charged it up to his disappointment at not finding his 'four footed girl friend', but not being sure, and trusting slightly in his instincts, we fed the ducks and decided not to hang around.

I wondered where Tony and his pooch were but wasn't worried. After all, we were extremely early. Moira had said Mutt was getting tired of just wandering around the block, and since Tony was usually early, I guess I'd just hoped they'd be here.

Now I was really going to have to hurry if I was going to pick up Susan and get to work on time.

Chris called me about 10:00 a.m., right during a particularly slow time. The breakfast customers had all left and we were gearing up toward the lunch hour. He stated that his Captain 'wouldn't mind' if the story got out. He'd even agree to be interviewed afterward. Good P.R. for the police department, I thought. Possibly also for himself, I thought. Politics are everywhere.

Anyway, having obtained permission to 'leak' the story I approached Susan and said:

"Hey, there, kid, we've talked about you making out your Will. Have you done it yet?"

Her reply was, "Yep. At least we started. I have to take a little time off this morning to go to my lawyer's office and sign it. I presume Angela can take over for me for about half an hour. She's done it before."

"Good. Let me know when you get back. I've got a plan I'd like to discuss with you. And it involves Gabby, if you don't object to it."

She said she trusted my instincts, so I called Gabby Gabrielle to invite her to an early lunch, on me. Naturally she was out, but I finally persuaded the receptionist to give me her cell phone number, on the grounds that it might be a good scoop.

"I can't make it by 11:30," she said, "Could we make it late? Like about 1:30? I could probably get there by that time."

We agreed on the time, and I went back to work, admittedly spending more time mulling over the dastardly plot which I had in mind than planning food purchases. Fortunately those were pretty much the same from week to week.

Susan returned, coming to the kitchen to report before taking up her duties in the dining room. "All done, Aunt Ellie. I feel like I've just joined the ranks of those needing to pre-plan my funeral."

"You've done exactly the opposite, honey. You've just avoided needing burial plot and casket any time soon," I told her.

Gabby arrived right on time, and she and Susan and I sat down at a corner table, away from the few remaining lunchers, and I unveiled my plot.

"Gabby," I said, "I don't know if you are aware of it, but Kathryn and I had an intruder at the house recently."

"I'd heard the rumor, but no details. Is there a scoop for me?"

"Might be. I've gotten permission to 'leak' the story.

"I reached home to face this strange fellow, with a bandana for a mask, dressed rather weirdly. He had a gun and his first words were 'where is she?'—then he stopped and demanded money instead.

"I was pretty much focused on the gun pointed my direction, but even then I was frankly kind of amused at the disguise, and I DID register the first question. I figured he was looking for Susan, since she'd stayed one night with us, and I was now driving her to and from work. He probably thought she still lived with us.

"Fortunately for me, Moira was home, heard us, and came out with her own little cannon, and we sort of captured him, tied him up with the dog leash, which Mutt had come out with, anticipating a walk. The whole thing was just plain weird. There's no other way to describe it, unless the word farce comes to mind.

"The police came, hauled him away, and now I've been told that he really was after Susan. He said there was a street rumor that she was worth $10,000. He was high on drugs and thought that was a goodly sum to fund his habit for a while.

"The comical part of it was that he had no idea where to deliver the goods and pick up his cash. He was just too spaced out to be making sense.

Gabby asked, "What about the street rumor? Is it true?"

"The police think it is, but haven't been able to trace it. So my idea is to give out the story, along with the information that Susan has made out her Will, so whoever made the offer will realize its futility."

Susan said, "And you think that makes me safe?"

"Safer anyway," I replied. "But we need to do this rather publicly. Gabby, you get the scoop, but can you manage to get it on the television news? I have a proposed script, but would gladly leave it up to you."

"I not only can, but I will. My husband is a TV cameraman, and my paper is affiliated with the TV station anyway. I can do the interview, he can film it, and get it on the evening news."

"Great!" I said, "When can we do it?"

She said, "I'll set it up and let you know. I'd like to catch the two of you arriving in the morning, and we can get it on tomorrow's news broadcasts. I'll call you this evening."

Her plan worked out, and they were standing at the door the following morning when we arrived for work.

It went something like this:

| | |
|---|---|
| Gabby: | "Miss Gianelli, is it true that there's a reward out for you? A hit, worth about $10,000?" |
| Susan: | "I've heard that, yes. Wouldn't that be a laugh?" |
| Gabby: | "A laugh? I don't see anything very funny about it." |
| Susan: | "I don't either, personally. But the university finance people would be laughing all the way to the bank if something happens to me." |
| Gabby: | "The University? Why?" |
| Susan: | "Because just yesterday I executed a Will leaving everything to them. One-fourth of it would be for scholarships for deserving students, but most of it goes to the University hospital for research. My mother died of cancer. So did Aunt Ellie's sister. I just wanted to do something to help other people. It's not limited to just cancer research however. There's MS, Juvenile Diabetes, lots of research going on that needs funding." |
| Gabby: | "How did you learn about this potential 'hit' and do you have any information as to who is behind it?" |

Susan then told the story of the intruder and what he'd told the police. Gabby asked what he'd been charged with, when would it come to Trial, etc., and we referred her to the Police Captain for further information and interview.

I figured this would make his day. Possibly he's up for a promotion to Chief or planning to run for Sheriff or something and could use the publicity. I'd already noticed he's a rather handsome and personable man and no doubt the women of the county would be lining up to vote for him!

I thanked Gabby and she said, "Any time. I'm always up for a good story. Trying to get on as crime reporter. I'd like to turn Gabby over to somebody else. I'm tired of her."

Gabby left.

Customers were lining up.

We opened up for the day.

In an effort to dispel the growing rumors of a serious rift between herself and her stepmother, Susan held another large 'family' party at the restaurant, and invited Eva.

I'd only seen Eva once before, when I'd attended the visitation for her husband, and she'd been rather heavily veiled.

Now I saw her as George Gianelli must have seen her, a very beautiful woman, glossy dark hair, fair clear skin, perfect features and body. About 5'7" tall and my best guess would be 135 pounds, she could only be called 'perfection', at least in appearance.

She arrived precisely on time, making no grand entrance such as Gabby Gabrielle was inclined to make, was very gracious and was escorted to her seat by Richard, who of course was familiar with her, as one of his patients.

She remembered me, which was a trifle surprising, since we'd only met the one time, and then under stressful circumstances.

She shook hands with everyone and kissed Susan lightly on the cheek. I give the girl credit. She returned the gesture with a slight, brief hug and inquired as to how Eva was getting along.

By the time the amenities were over and our orders taken, Gabby swooshed in, but didn't approach our table, having chosen another victim, if I may call them that, to attack.

I wasn't particularly worried about them. We'd given Gabby prior notice, both of the party, and names of other possible guests, and she'd told me they loved the attention, and quite often deliberately set out to obtain it.

I considered it a 'win-win' situation for everyone concerned. Gabby got her column. Eva was seen by many people, socializing amicably with her stepdaughter, and the other people got noticed for the evening.

Richard proved to be the entertainment for the evening. I'd never noticed how clever and witty he could be when he turned on the charm.

Norma of course had to check on the status of the greyhound that had been with George at the time of his death, and found Eva willing to talk about it. Either she or one of her brothers was walking their two dogs every day, but she did think the one in particular missed George. "Dogs do have feelings, I'm convinced of that. He occasionally goes in George's office and sits by his desk, as if trying to find out why his buddy isn't there. He was George's favorite. The other one, frankly prefers to hang out with the chauffeur. He's lazy but likes to ride."

"He'll get over it," said Norma, "Just give him plenty of attention."

"We do." was Eva's reply.

Kat and Moira and I went home considering the evening to be a success, and worth doing, but wondered if it would bring on a repeat dinner.

Probably not, was my conclusion.

I returned home Wednesday afternoon and headed for the stairway, intending to change from work clothes into jeans and t-shirt to go to the back yard and play frisbee with Mutt. He was needing some attention other than walking around the block. That was MY opinion, of course. I don't pretend to know what HE was thinking. I needed the exercise, so had decided he did too.

Before I could get my foot on the first step, Moira came from the kitchen, "Hey, Ellie, hold up. I've got news!"

"From???" I asked.

"From Patrick, of course."

"By telephone or in print?" was my question.

"Why? What's the difference?"

I said, "Because if you printed it out, why can't I just take it upstairs with me and read it?"

"Because I'm too excited about it to wait."

"Okay," I replied, "Let's go back to the kitchen and put on the coffee."

"I already made some."

So we sat at the kitchen table, nibbled on carrot sticks (I simply MUST start cutting back. I've been eating too much rich food at the restaurant), and Mutt sat at my feet wagging his tale while Moira told her tail. (Must I re-write that? Spell-check doesn't seem to object)

"I've been curious," she said, "and asked Patrick to do some checking. He's so much more proficient at it than I am.

"Anyway, I'd picked up a rumor that Eva's marriage to Gianelli was her second, and wondered just how the first one ended? Divorce? Knife in the gut? Poison? Natural death?

"Anyway, Patrick found the record of not only one, but two previous marriages. The first one had a record of death, only a couple of months prior to her marriage to the second guy.

"But he couldn't find any record of either death or divorce from this fellow."

"You mean he's still out there somewhere? Still married to Eva?"

"Very probably. And that would mean, of course, that she wasn't legally Mrs. George Gianelli!"

"Wow!" I exclaimed, "Go on, Moira, what's the rest of the story?"

"Patrick found several men of the same name. He's eliminated a couple, but two are worth investigating, if Shell would authorize some trips."

"I'll ask her, but I'm sure she would," I said, heading for the phone.

She stopped me, "Wait, Ellie, that's not quite all. Patrick thinks the older man, about 58 years old, is probably the father of the second, who is only 32. Both of them reside in New Mexico."

"Wow again!" I said, "That could mean Eva has a son?"

"Patrick seems to think that's a possibility." Moira replied. "Now you can call Shell."

Shell, of course, said, "I'll call Abe immediately. Julie can fly him to New Mexico tonight yet if they can get together on flight time."

I took the e-mail print-out upstairs with me to read the details, then got into my 'grubbies' and Mutt and I went to play.

He wore me out and was reluctant to quit. I wasn't. I'm not as young as he is!

That wasn't all my niece had to say.

"You sound like you are getting all weirded out, Aunt Ellie. I suggest you go talk to somebody about all this."

"Tony?" I asked.

"No," she said, "Richard."

Which is why Thursday afternoon found me taking a chance on catching the good Dr. Banks between patients. His office was only a few blocks from the restaurant, so I left my car in the parking lot and walked over.

His receptionist said "He has a patient at the moment, but she'll be leaving soon. I'm sure he could give you a few minutes, if you'd care to wait?"

I waited.

Richard walked his young patient to the door, saying, "Now you go home and think about this. And DO NOT go blabbing to your best friend. She's part of your problem. If you intend to keep her as a best friend, she's got to stay out of your personal life for a while. Are you hearing me?"

She nodded and left. He turned to me, "What's up, Eleanor?"

We went into his private office, closed the door, sat down, and I silently handed him Abe's latest information. "He left for New Mexico late yesterday to try to check these two men out," I told him, after he'd read the message.

"You do realize this could change everything, if it turns out to be true?" he asked.

"Yep. It changes a lot. There are now new suspects to consider, if either or both of them had decided to help Eva out, possibly for a pay-off. There's also now the possibility that Eva would not inherit anything from Gianelli's estate, if the marriage doesn't exist. I don't think she or her family would appreciate that one bit!

"We do have to consider Susan. Do we tell her, or wait until Abe gets more information?"

He said, "Let me make a copy of this. I'll think about it, and try to figure out what, or how much, to tell her.

"I think her estate attorney should also be made aware of this possibility before any disposition of assets is made."

I asked, "But Susan is the one who would have to talk to him, isn't she? He represents her. We don't have any stake in this game."

"I'll talk to her tonight," he promised, "I'll just make another copy of this report for her to give him."

This also makes me wonder what exactly exactly what happened to Husband No. One. I'd like to know the cause of death.

And so we went back to waiting.

AGAIN!

My little friend was strangely quiet the next morning. She did her work as efficiently as usual, but reminded me of a robot, simply programmed for the job.

At 9:00 a.m. she picked up her purse and said, "Can you manage by yourself for about an hour? I've got an appointment with my attorney."

"Uh huh," was my response.

"You know why?"

I repeated my Uh huh and she left.

An hour later she was back, rushing straight through to the office. She looked upset so I followed her, "You okay, honey?"

Her eyes were red from crying, but they always were after any visit or conversation that reminded her of her father. Grief goes away slowly, and she hadn't yet had enough time for that to happen.

I merely said, "There's not much going on at the moment, honey. I'll take care of the kitchen. You sit here and catch up on paper work. Okay?"

"Uh huh."

Did she pick that up from me, or does the whole world mess up the English language? I'd tried to keep Shell grammatically correct, after Mother was gone and couldn't do it any longer, but keep noticing my lack of success. Shell says uh huh too. Plus a lot of other commonly used slang expressions.

Nobody would ever know from listening to us that Mother once taught English and Literature!

Susan's attorney had instructed us to say nothing about Eva's marital status, but, in his words, "Just sit on it until Mr. Abrams comes down from his mountain and presents us with his report carved in stone. Then we will talk about it further".

So that's what we did, although it was difficult. I was simply dying to 'leak' another story to Gabby—she'd really love this one. I'd want a lot more coverage on it than just Gabby & husband, but thought she'd be willing to share the glory for a story this big. Provided it proved true, of course.

My gut instincts told me it was, but who wants to get sued?

It was a long week-end. Moira checked her e-mail almost hourly. The suspense was getting to all of us.

Fortunately other events occurred to distract us—

Monday morning arrived, and with it a middle-aged couple. Susan introduced them, saying, "I think we are letting you retire at the end of the week, Aunt Ellie. I'm trying to convince Gerald and Joan to transfer here from another of our restaurants."

"That's great," I exclaimed, "Oh, Susan, I didn't mean it to sound quite like I'm anxious to leave. I've really had fun here, but I guess I'm spoiled. I've never had to punch a clock or keep regular hours—not since Shell was little and I had to get her off to school. Freedom to do what I want, when and where I want, is what I like best."

They I added, "And then what do THEY do? The other restaurant, I mean?"

Gerald answered, "There are a couple of promotions due over there, and they will simply hire a couple of new people for their positions. It would work out very well."

"Golly," I said, "If you are selling a house and hunting for a new one, I can refer you to a great realtor."

Susan said, "I was about to suggest that myself."

Gerald and Joan, having inspected the restaurant, decided they'd love to move. "I've always liked this city," was Joan's decision, "Show us your realtor."

We promptly called Kathryn and invited her to lunch. "Drumming up business," is what I told her.

*Dear Shelly,*

*I can never thank you enough for the 'loan' of Moira, and for all the work Patrick has done.*

*Golly, I never noticed, but I guess all these days, weeks now, of association with Moira have rubbed off on me. I'm now calling 'Abe' Patrick, just like his mother does.*

*I think Moira is beginning to be anxious about getting home again and just doesn't want to say so, since the murder of George Gianelli is still unsolved.*

*Susan and I no longer feel that there is any risk to either of us, so if she wants to leave I'll understand. Also, although we've loved having her, I suspect Kat is also getting ready to have our house, and our lives, back.*

*I'd hoped to show Moira the sights, entertain her at least a little while she's here, but circumstances seem to have put a kink in my plans.*

*I've ended up working an eight hour shift at the restaurant, and she seems to be spending most of her time either in her room staring at her laptop, or dragging it downstairs with her, apparently anticipating more information from Patrick.*

*The new manager and his wife are starting work next Monday, even if they have to either commute or find a motel or short term rental apartment, so I'll be free.*

*Perhaps if Patrick can spare his Mom another week I can make it up to her. There are lots of things to see, and do, that I believe she'd enjoy.*

*In the meantime, thanks again. I can never repay you, except with my*

*Love, Aunt Ellie*

Shell answered:

*Dearest Aunt Ellie,*

*You've got it all wrong. It's I who can never repay YOU!*

*I never forget that you gave up your life, your hopes, your dreams, your education, and even the years you and Kathryn might have had together, to take care of a child that wasn't even yours!*

*Anything you ever need, if it's in my power to give it to you, I will do it. I'll love you forever.*

*Your substitute child, Shell*

I finally stopped crying and decided it was time for a long walk. Mutt had been patiently and sympathetically sitting on my foot. I had to bang it on the floor a few times to wake it up!

I turned off my computer. He took that as a 'walk' message and came with his leash. I stuffed my pocket with plastic baggies and we left.

It was nearly noon when Moira came rushing into the restaurant. Susan found her a table and had a waiter get her some coffee while she waited for us to be free to join her. It was difficult to pay proper attention to the customers, as it was obvious she was excited about something.

We finally joined her, taking lunch for the three of us, not bothering to ask her what she'd like to have.

"Okay, Moira, what's up?"

She hauled several papers from her purse and put them before us. Patrick had located Robert Gleeson and his son, Robert, Jr. The elder Robert admitted having married Eva Ryker Adams and that the son was Eva's child.

They had many marital problems, most of them apparently due to interference from Eva's family, but had remained together until the child was two years old.

He'd come home from work one day to find the child alone in the house, hungry, wet and dirty in his playpen, and is mother nowhere in sight.

He'd thought his first priority was to search the house to see if Eva was sick or injured and couldn't find her. His next job was to clean and feed the boy, then he'd gone searching for evidence of where Eva might have gone.

All her clothes were gone from the closet and her jewelry box was missing. He'd called the police, who found no evidence that the house had been broken into or that a struggle had ensued. They concluded she'd simply left and pursued it no further.

The next day he'd checked the bank and discovered he and the son had nothing left except the house, its remaining contents, and the cash in his pocket. Luckily he had a pretty good job, the mortgage, utilities and insurance had already been paid, and they simply survived until the next payday and whatever food was left in the refrigerator and freezer.

He'd then decided to count his blessings and make a satisfactory life for himself and his child.

She'd cleaned them out, but they were better off without the continuous hassle, both with Eva and with her family.

He'd never filed for divorce. Neither had he ever been served papers from her or her attorneys, nor had he made any attempt to locate her, although he knew where the family lived. He wanted nothing from her, and nothing more to do with any of the Rykers.

He'd survived, educated his son, they were both happy and that's all that mattered to him.

This was pretty much the basics of Patrick's report, although there were details, dates, etc., that Susan's attorney might want.

I got out my cell phone and called Gabby, "Have I got another scoop to 'leak'. Get yourself over to the restaurant as fast as you can!"

It took her less than ten minutes!

At six o'clock the following morning we found the parking lot full of cars and vans, and Susan was immediately bombarded with cameras, microphones and screaming reporters, Gabby and her husband leading the pack.

I hope and trust nobody saw her wink at me as she shouted, "Miss Gianelli, is it true that your stepmother wasn't legally married to your father?"

Others were shoving their microphones forward, shouting questions-

"Is it true....?"

"What does this mean to her inheritance...."

"MISS GIANELLI....'

It was a real rat race to see who could get close to Susan. I was enjoying myself immensely. Susan simply kept shoving her way toward the door, keys in hand.

Finally she turned and said, "I really don't know, and I don't want to discuss it with you. If there is something to report I presume you will find out. In the meantime, I have a business to run and an appointment to make with my attorney. Please excuse me."

We managed to get inside and re-lock the door. Until legitimate customers started arriving it would remain that way.

A few minutes later my cell phone rang.

Gabby said, "Thanks, Eleanor. If this keeps up I may yet get transferred from gossip to the crime beat. Anything else happening?"

"If I have anything new I know where to find you." I said.

"Okay. Thanks again. Keep in touch."

What I'd failed to tell her was what Patrick had found about Eva's first husband. He'd been found shot to death. The bullet had entered his left temple, the unregistered gun lying by his left hand.

Initially the police had wondered about this, but the distraught widow had stated her husband was left-handed, and friends confirmed this. They'd closed the case after listing it as suicide.

Now they were re-opening the case.

I didn't intend to tell Gabby this. I've noticed that reporters make some of the best detectives in the world, and I was certain they'd start doing their own research. They might even come up with more than Patrick had found. There might be a real rat-race for the scoop.

In the meantime, although the murder of Susan's father had not been solved, I was beginning to get my life back, and was giving serious thought to Gabby's suggestion of writing either a food column, or the interviews with senior citizens, or possibly both, depending on what time I wanted to spend on it, and her Editor's decision.

Mutt was tugging persistently on his leash. Yeah. Again. He was delighted to be getting back to our old routine. I was equally happy.

Susan seemed to be safe and would be off to college soon. The restaurant was under new management. Kat had found temporary housing for the new managers as they sought something permanent. They had a prospective buyer for their previous home. I was back to cooking for fun, and for friends and family, not for picky customers, not that I'd had any complaints, but surely sooner or later someone would gripe about their steak being overdone or their coffee too weak!

True, the murder of George Gianelli had not been solved, but on this bright and sunny morning somehow that didn't seem to matter. Let the police worry about that!

Tony had beaten me to the duck pond. I plunked myself down beside him, helped myself to his donut and coffee bag and turned Mutt loose, hoping I could trust him not to run off. His time with Moira seemed to have paid off and he was behaving much better now. If she ever decides to give up detective work perhaps she could become a dog trainer. I'd told her so.

Two bites into my cream filled long john Chris came running full speed, not a bit out of breath, as I would have been. So much for youth vs age.

"What's up?" I asked, "Why the big rush?"

"Got news." he replied.

Tony was nodding. I reckoned that meant he knew the answer to my 'what's up' question, and I glared at him for not warning me. He just grinned back at me and said nothing.

"We arrested Kenneth Ryker this morning for the murder of his sister's husband!" exclaimed the young cop.

"That's great!" I spluttered through some of the gooey cream filling, "At least, I reckon it's great. That is if he's guilty. But what about that menacing looking guy he hangs around with all the time? Is he arrested too?"

I searched in my pockets for a tissue to mop the goo off my face and could only seem to come up with unused doggy-doo plastic bags.

Tony silently handed me his handkerchief. "You'll get this back after I do laundry," I told him.

He still said nothing.

Chris finally asked, "What's the matter, Judge?"

"I don't believe he did it." was Tony's response.

"Why? There's plenty of evidence," said Chris.

"What evidence? The knife came from the restaurant. Any employee or customer could have carried one off. It was, after all, just a common steak knife—comes with all the steaks and chops."

I asked, "What about all the intimidation they seemed to be putting on Susan? I'd call that a little bit incriminating."

"Not a bit," he said, "That came AFTER the fact, just trying to push Eva's interests in the estate and scare Susan into backing off. Nothing to do with the murder."

Chris asked, "Then why don't you consider him to be guilty?"

"He hasn't got the guts!" He handed the rest of the donuts to Chris, put Duchess back on her leash, and walked away, leaving us bewildered and with egg on our faces, so to speak. Of course mine was really cream filling. We finished off the donuts, cheating the ducks.

*Dear Shell,*

*Free at last! Well, not exactly free, but at least from my 6 to 2 shift at Gianellis. I've discussed the column and actually went to the local retirement home to 'visit' with some of the old folks there. They have a lot of interesting stories to tell, and it really would be fun to collect some of them, along with old recipes and cooking habits, into a column. I think I have enough talent to write them up, and if not, that's an idea I'll just have to give up and go back to my original thought of doing my own cookbook.*

*Mutt actually decided to 'heel' all the way home from the park this morning. I rewarded him with an extra doggy treat, in hopes he'll remember that tomorrow.*

*Enough said about me and the pooch.*

*Just wanted to report that the police arrested Kenneth Ryker for murder and that Tony doesn't think he's guilty. He just walked off this morning with no explanation, and left my big curiousity bump bigger than ever. Maybe he'll come clean tomorrow.*

*Love, Aunt Ellie.*

Next morning:

*Dear Aunt Ellie,*

*Thanks for keeping us in the loop. Joe and Mac have run off to Texas, leaving Leeanna and I to fend for ourselves.*

*They wanted to check up on some of Rayburn Enterprises industries down there, including the truck farm Rudy Garcia is running. Dad called in last night and reported that it's going well and he's pleased with the 'looks' of the place as well as the 'looks' of the financial statistics.*

*As to the judge and his doubts, it's very likely he's had some experiences with the Ryker family in years gone by and has greater insights into the capabilities and characteristics of some of them than even the police have.*

*Keep reporting in. I like to know what's going on in your life.*

*I love you, Shell*

Well, I did it. My first story goes to print tomorrow, and getting it was a most enjoyable experience.

I'd gone along with Norma on one of her trips to a residential facility where she regularly takes Charlie for visits with the elderly. They love him, and he's so well-behaved, it makes me hope Mutt gets some manners so I could take him places like that.

Using Gabby's suggestion, I thought while we were there I could stop and interview someone, but I never got inside the door.

Sitting on a bench on the patio was a little but spritely white-haired lady with a small garden trowel in her hand, brushing dirt from her clothes.

I sat down beside her and asked what she'd been doing.

"Oh, just digging a few weeds from the flower beds. Nobody minds if I putter and it's good exercise. I've always loved gardening."

We talked for quite some time. I learned where she was from, all about her family, and present life here at the residence.

She caught me looking at her petite little feet encased in purple sandals, at the end of a pair of still shapely legs and she said, "Oh, I know purple shoes don't go well with kelly green shorts, but I got mud on my tennies and these are rubber. I can just turn the hose on them and wait until they dry enough to go back inside.

If I find more people like Rosie, this job is going to be a lot of fun!

Days turned into weeks. Susan left for college. Kat had found permanent housing for the restaurant managers and Chris seemed to be around more and more—an accepted member of the Banks family. Deeanna went around humming softly and I wondered if she was choosing wedding songs, but didn't ask. She was now sporting a lovely ring and waving it around in front of all our noses.

We continued to entertain at the house occasionally, Kat saying I didn't need to lose any of my culinary skills, but for the most part the family gatherings were held at Gianellis, thus allowing those who didn't care to entertain at home to be able to attend and still feel guilt-free.

Tony still had not elaborated on why he considered Kenneth Ryker to be innocent, but apparently he was not in jail, either released or out on bail, I didn't know which.

I'd written several articles for my "The Way it Was" column, and so far the editors hadn't thrown me out on my ear. I had a few compliments on it, but since most of those were from friends and relatives, I took them with the proverbial grain of salt.

Kat said nobody but people close to us would know who "Aunt Ellie" was, but I might as well expect people to begin to recognize me on the street, since my picture (tiny but rather good, I thought) was included in the heading.

And I really was enjoying my visits with the charming senior citizens of Charlotte.

We were gathered around our favorite table at the restaurant when Susan rushed in. She appeared to be extremely upset and confused.

"Honey," I exclaimed, "What's wrong? Why are you home?"

"That's what I want to know," she said, "Chris sent a message that I was to be here, tonight, without fail, so here I am!"

Chris looked at Tony. Tony looked at Richard. Richard looked at Chris.

I yelled at all three of them, loud enough to get a few odd looks from neighboring tables, "Well, is one of you going to say something?"

It was Richard who took up the challenge, "Susan, honey, we didn't want you to hear it on TV or read it in the paper, but Eva has been arrested for your father's murder."

"What?"

Tony pushed his chair over to make space, pulled in another from the next table, pointed to it and said, "Better sit down, honey."

She didn't sit. She collapsed.

Richard shoved an untouched glass of water toward her and said, "Take a sip, child, and prepare yourself for a story."

"I'm okay, I guess," she said, "But why Eva? I thought Kenneth had been charged with it already. That part didn't surprise me much. He's such a creep!"

"So is Eva, apparently," muttered Chris.

Helen broke in, "Tony, dear, I think you've got some explaining to do."

"Right," he said, "It's like this Susan. The case sort of broke wide open when a gas station manager came strolling into police headquarters with a credit card receipt, signed by Eva Gianelli. His station is about half way to Atlanta, where she was located after her husband's body was found, and the date and time stamped on it belied the time-table she and her alibi witness had provided.

"Further investigation, and interrogation of her so-called witness, and her alibi fell apart. He admitted lying, and also stated that Eva told him she'd killed her husband, that she'd inherit a large estate, and he'd share it with her. He just had to stick with his story.

"She'd told him George had been 'making divorce' noises lately, and a pre-nup she'd signed years ago would have left her penniless."

"Why was he going to divorce her after all these years?" asked Susan.

"Seems he was tired of her cheating. He knew about this guy in Atlanta. He was also tired of the constant fighting about money and decided it was time to get out of a bad arrangement, cut his losses, possibly pay alimony for a while, but that was about all she'd get. That's when she decided to simply bump him off and 'Go directly to cash' on the board game of life. So now she's incarcerated, Kenneth is free, as I'd anticipated. I knew from past experiences with him that he's all bluster and no guts. Also, he's just not the brightest bulb in his family's chandelier."

I said, "So it's over at last?"

"All over but the trial, which is going to be rather messy, so we (indicating Chris and Richard) thought we ought to advise Susan in advance."

*Dear Shell,*

*Since I've told you about Eva's arrest, thought I'd catch you up on a few details, but first, thanks again for the loan of Moira. She was a delightful guest and we miss her, although I must admit it's nice to get back to our regular existence, just Kat, Mutt and Me.*

*Speaking of cats, I've been seriously considering getting a kitten or two, but am not sure how Mutt will react.*

*Oh, before I forget, thanks also for Abe's assistance. Without his information many of Susan's problems would remain unresolved.*

*She's contacted the relatives and met some of them. She, of course, is now in college, but took an apartment near the restaurant, in order to have her own place when she's in town, or during breaks.*

*With Eva out of the picture, both as to the illegality of her marriage to Gianelli, and by reason of her incarceration, of course Susan now gets the house and balance of her father's estate. Kat has put the big house on the market for her, since she insists it holds only bad, and sad memories for her, and very few good ones.*

*She worried about the two dogs, but Richard and Norma took one, and Tony and Helen took the other. Both report the respective pooches doing well without their old friend, and with their new one, so all's well on that score.*

*Chris and Deeanna are making 'marriage' noises, so presumably Norma will soon be having a wonderful time helping with wedding plans. I hope to be asked to cater, and if I'm NOT, I'll be seriously annoyed. I've instructed Kat to so inform her niece, and state that I'm volunteering to supply everything, including the cake.*

*Hug Leeanna for me.*

*Love, Aunt Ellie*

*Dear Aunt Ellie,*

*Consider Leeanna hugged.*

*Consider yourself totally welcome to services of Moira and Abe.*

*And consider the kittens. Mitch gets along famously with Lucky, and we've taken in a cute calico kitten from a litter Jake found in the barn. Lucky's nose was out of joint for only a couple of days, then he decided it was his. Probably not!*

*Love, Shell*

"I have a dilemma."

"A serious one?" asked Tony as he unleashed Duchess and handed me a donut from his bag and tossed another to the ducks.

"Afraid so," was my reply, "And I don't know what to do about it. It may be better to do absolutely nothing. But it's going to continue to hang around like a nuclear bomb ready to pop at any moment."

He said, "I don't think nuclear bombs pop. However I'm your lawyer. Client confidentiality and all that stuff, if you want to tell me and get it off your mind."

So I told him my story, accompanied by an occasional tear.

"When I was fifteen I attended a party one evening with a bunch of classmates. Pop didn't want me to go, but I guess I bullied Mom and she said okay as long as I got home by midnight.

"It was at the home of one of the town's prominent citizens, and given by their son and daughter. Having arrived, I found the kids all there alone. The parents had gone off for a three day trip somewhere, and the kids took advantage of it.

"I didn't like the tone of the party from the start, but frankly I didn't get much beyond that start. Somebody handed me a drink, allegedly non-alcoholic, and I remember very little after that.

"I remember feeling a little dizzy and made an excuse to go to the kitchen and get some pizza, thinking food might help.

"At least that was the excuse. Actually my intent was to sneak out the back door and walk home.

"I don't even remember reaching the kitchen. The next thing I did remember was waking up in the hospital the next day.

"Mom was semi-hysterical, and Pops was obviously ready to blast somebody off the face of the earth. He wasn't usually that way, actually very mild mannered, but not this time.

"He'd stayed up, waiting for me, heard a vehicle in the driveway and reached the door in time to see me being dumped out of the car onto the concrete. He was too upset to even think of getting the license number, or even call 911—just picked me up and rushed to the hospital.

"The doctors of course reported it, said I'd been raped, probably by several persons, but since it happened at the home of one of the town's most prominent citizens, it got hushed up and no charges were ever filed.

"Pops was furious, and when it turned out that I was pregnant I managed to finish the school year without anyone being the wiser. I was always a trifle chunky, not really fat, but a LONG way from skinny, and with some baggy clothes, which everybody was wearing anyway, I got away with it and as soon as school was out I went to Charlotte and stayed with my grandmother. We all hoped the baby would arrive before the next school session, and it did, just a few days before.

"I'd signed the adoption papers, gone shopping to try to keep occupied, and that's when Kat found me in front of the shoe store.

"I've never told anyone this before, not even Kat."

Tony asked, "And the father was?"

"We never found out. It could have been any one of half a dozen boys who were there. When asked why I was dumped in the driveway all the kids said I'd gotten sick at the party and they decided to take me home. They insisted everyone thought I was all right, but of course that was a big fat lie!"

"We could still find out. Line up all the boys, now grown men of course, and get DNA testing. That is if you know who adopted the child so we could get it from him. Or HER?."

I mopped some more tears, with Tony's ever present handkerchief and said, "It's HIM. I didn't know who took him. Not at the time at least."

"And now something has happened to change that?"

"Yes. I think I knew immediately, and with some investigating by Moira and her son, I know for certain."

Tony replied, "Ellie, honey, I told you my son was adopted—but he's not…."

"Oh, I know that."

"Because Helen and I know the mother of our son. We keep in touch with her, and so does he."

"But now that I know, I don't know what to do about it. I'm not even sure he's aware of having been adopted. His mother, I'm fairly certain, knows, but I just can't walk up to her and say "Thank you for raising my child", can I?"

"That depends, I guess, on who it is," said Tony.

"Well, then I guess I can't. And I really don't know what I should do."

He took my hand, looked me square in the eyes and replied, "I suggest you discuss this with Richard. He could probably help you, if not to resolve the problem itself, but to make you feel better about it."

"Richard? Oh, NO. I couldn't possibly do that."

"Why not? Just hand him a dollar. Patient confidentiality and all that. Just like you have client confidentiality with me."

I actually giggled at that, "I never gave you a dollar."

"But I come pro bono, so that's okay."

"Well, anyway, I still can't tell Richard."

"I repeat. Why not?"

"Because of Deeanna, of course."

"Deanna?" he exclaimed, "What in the world has she got to do with it?"

I replied "Because she's going to marry him, of course. Oh, Tony, you aren't usually so dense. It's Chris, of course."

Chris Marchand is my son.

978-0-595-47632-9
0-595-47632-5

4212194

Made in the USA
Lexington, KY
05 January 2010